Cattle Drive to Dodge

Other Avalon Books by Kent Conwell

PANHANDLE GOLD

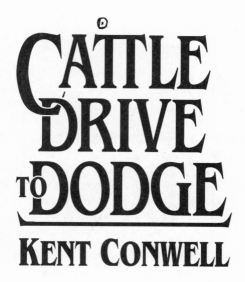

CATTLE DRIVE TO DODGE

KENT CONWELL

AVALON BOOKS
THOMAS BOUREGY AND COMPANY, INC.
401 LAFAYETTE STREET
NEW YORK, NEW YORK 10003

PRINTED IN THE UNITED STATES OF AMERICA
ON ACID-FREE PAPER
BY HADDON CRAFTSMEN, SCRANTON, PENNSYLVANIA

To Mom and Dad, for discipline and love.

And to Gayle.

Chapter One

When I was six, Ned Cooper bought me from the Colorado Utes for six beavers and one bearskin. He named me Shadrach Colter and raised me on a small spread cradled among the blue mountains far to the West. There, he taught me the skills that a man needs to survive on the frontier. I grew up rawhide tough and red-oak solid. All primed for grizzly, I had more brawn than sense early on.

After Ned passed on, a strange restlessness came over me, one I had trouble explaining, but one I hoped to still by putting down my roots and building a life for myself.

Ned claimed that he gave me the name Shadrach because I always went looking for the fiery furnace of trouble. But I never did. Trouble just somehow happened to be wherever I reined in for the night.

But that old man's somber declaration came true once again in Sweetwater Creek, a small town on the banks of the gentle stream from which it drew its name. Typical of most small towns in the West, the village's main street was lined with false-fronted buildings and whitewashed adobe.

I rode into town on a blistering-hot summer afternoon and pulled up in front of the local saloon. My mouth was set for an ice-cold beer, but I figured I would have to settle for just a wet one since a small town like Sweetwater Creek probably wouldn't have ice until winter.

I climbed off my buckskin, and I had just flipped the reins around the hitching rail when a harsh voice called out: "Hey! You there! Hold on!"

I paid the voice no mind. I knew no one in town, so there was no way anyone could be speaking to me. I stomped up on the boardwalk, slapped my slouch hat against my leg to knock off some dust, and started through the batwing doors. Suddenly, a handful of fingers dug into my arm and spun me around.

A young man wearing a pair of Colts faced me. He had a frown on his sunburned face and a star pinned to his shirt. "Didn't you hear me, cowboy? I said for you to hold on."

Behind him stood two other young cowpokes, each with a sneering grin on his face. A cigarette dangled from the lips of one of them.

"You talking to me?" I asked.

"Yeah, you. I don't see nobody else around here, do you?"

His manner was rough and downright irritating, and I knew at once he was used to throwing his weight around, especially in front of his friends. But I put a tight rein on my temper and said, "Sorry, Sheriff. I'm new in town and I didn't figure on anybody bothering to talk to me."

One of the cowboys snickered, and the young man's face reddened. He hooked a thumb at the star on his chest. "Deputy sheriff, cowboy." His voice grew louder. "I reckon you can read, can't you?"

Townsfolk on the sidewalk looked around to see what the commotion was all about. Three or four edged closer. I felt my ears burning, not so much from embarrassment as from holding my temper in check. I'd been around long enough to know when someone was spoiling for a fight. "Okay, Deputy, what can I do for you?"

He glanced over his shoulder at the two rowdies behind him and gave them a smug grin. He turned back to me. "What's your business in town?"

A buckboard stopped in the middle of the dusty street to watch the one-sided quarrel.

I shrugged. "Just passing through."

He eyed me carefully. I knew what he was seeing—a lanky drink of water, a mite under six feet, wearing typical Western clothes: denim trousers, muslin shirt, and cotton vest. His eyes lingered on the well-oiled .44 on my hip. To him, I was no different from any other drifting cowpoke, and he probably figured he would treat me just as he did the others. He nodded. "Well, see that you do. We don't want no saddle tramps to bother the good people here in Sweetwater Creek."

We stood eye to eye. At his last words, I cut my eyes to the two cowpokes behind him. The one with the cigarette blew out a stream of smoke. I looked back at the deputy and grinned. I was going to behave just like old Ned had always told me—keep my thoughts to myself and just let the deputy's words roll right off my back. But it was hard, and I couldn't resist saying, "Whatever you say, Deputy. I can plainly see you don't allow riffraff on your streets here. Soon as I wet my whistle, I'll be moving on out of your fine little town."

One of the townspeople snickered. The deputy's face grew red. I nodded and turned back to the saloon.

His sharp words and the sound of a gun shucking leather stopped me before I'd taken two steps. "No, you ain't."

I looked back at him, taking care to keep my arms extended on either side, so that he and everyone else could plainly see I had no intention of going for my gun.

He motioned to my buckskin with the muzzle of his Colt. "You ain't wettin' your whistle nowhere in our town. You're forking leather and moving on now."

Before I could reply, one of the townsfolk spoke up: "All the man wants is a beer, Red. That won't hurt none." The man was pudgy and balding and he wore a white apron. One of the local merchants, I figured.

"Go on back and mind your groceries, Frank. I know his kind. Treat 'em good and they'll steal you blind when you ain't looking."

The merchant replied, "The sheriff don't like you badgering folks, Red. He's said so before."

Red snorted. "Newt told me to take care of things while he was gone, Frank. That's what I'm doing. Now stop interfering with the law." He waved the muzzle of his Colt impatiently in the direction of my horse. "You hear me, cowboy? Climb back on that mangy buckskin."

I drew in a deep breath, trying to cool the anger building up inside. No sense in losing my temper over a beer, but at the same time I didn't cotton to being pushed around, and I was right at the breaking point.

"Look, Deputy, I'm not causing any trouble. I'm here to spend some money. Then I'm riding out. Believe me, I've got no more desire to hang around your town than you have for me to be here."

As I said, any fool could see the deputy was spoiling for a fight, but if you looked closer, beneath the star, you could see a frightened boy who figured that jerking leather was the only way to prove he was a man. The glower in his eyes had given way to uncertainty. They darted from face to face in the crowd and settled on me. He drew the tip of his tongue across his dry lips. He was growing nervous—and dangerous.

As he shook his head, a nervous tic twisted his lips into a snarl. "You got no choice. Now beat it."

I studied him a moment, then decided to move on. He wasn't worth the trouble I'd make for myself if I taught him a lesson. With a shrug, I took a step toward my horse.

When I walked past him, he laughed and put his hand on my shoulder to give me a push toward my buckskin. When his hand touched my shoulder, I forgot all my solemn promises. I spun to my left and slapped his gun hand aside and whacked him alongside his head with the muzzle of my .44. He sagged.

In one swift motion, I bent my knees and slid my shoulder into his stomach and hefted him easily onto my back and turned my gun on the two rowdies with him. "Don't move a muscle, boys," I warned.

They froze. The one with the cigarette blinked against the smoke burning his eyes.

"Drop your belts."

The townsfolk took a step back. I glanced at the balding merchant after the gun belts hit the sidewalk. "I don't want any trouble, mister. Just point me at the jail. I'm putting these yahoos where they can't bother peaceable citizens for a spell, at least until I get out of this town of yours."

When the merchant realized what I had in mind, a wide grin split his face. "Across the street right over there, stranger."

I gestured toward the jail with the muzzle of my .44. "Okay, boys. Let's go."

The one with the cigarette dangling from his lips started to lower his hand. "Keep it up," I said. "Unless all you want is a stump on the end of that arm."

"But the cigarette is burning my lips."

"Spit it out then, but don't let those hands drop."

"It's stuck to my lip."

"Tough."

The cigarette burned his lip. He sputtered and spit and dragged his tongue over his lips, but he didn't drop his hands.

The townspeople traipsed after me. The merchant said, "My name's Frank Bevers. I own the grocery and dry goods store if you need anything, mister."

Five minutes later I had the three locked up tight in the adobe jail. The rowdy with the burned lip glared at me. "I'll get you for this, cowboy," he snarled. He looked to be about eighteen or nineteen, trying his best to be a man, but ignorant of how to go about such a job.

"Son," I told him, "I've seen the elephant and come back. Your kind is the last of my worries."

The second rowdy sat on the cot, his eyes fixed on the floor.

The merchant and a handful of other citizens had followed me into the jail and were treating me as if I were some kind of hero, which made me wonder about the kind of law around Sweetwater Creek.

I figured that the smartest move on my part now was to light a shuck out of town. I wanted to be a good piece away from there when the sheriff returned and freed the deputy and his mates. But I was too late. No sooner had I stepped outside the jail than a rider pulled up at the hitching rail. The star on his chest told me all I needed to know about him. He looked down from his saddle as we filed out of his jail.

"What the deuce is goin' on here?" he roared.

The man wearing the apron spoke up: "It was Red, Newt. He got out of hand, and this cowboy here cooled him off."

Newt Adams swung down. He was a tree stump of a man, blocky and square, and a web of blue veins on his face gave away his drinking habits. "The devil you say." He glared at me. "What do you say to that, cowboy?"

While I explained just what had happened, three or four more townsfolk came up, one dressed in a three-piece suit and wearing a black, flat-crowned Stetson, a hat that looked out of place with such a fine suit. I glanced past the sheriff and saw that the buckboard was still in the middle of the street. An old man and a young woman watched from the seat.

But most of the time, I kept my eyes on the sheriff, trying to read what he was thinking behind those blood-shot eyes. When I finished with my explanation, the merchant spoke up: "You see, Newt, it was like I said. This feller was minding his own business. Red just got carried away."

The tall man in the fine clothes shook his head. "That might be, Frank, but the way I understand it, the law is the law. Red is a legally appointed deputy." He paused and looked at me, his eyes cold and un-feeling, almost deadly. "Just because this gent or some other saddle bum happens to disagree with the law doesn't give him the right to strike a deputy uncon-scious."

Sheriff Adams nodded vigorously. "Mr. Perkins is right. We all got to obey the law." He looked around at me. "A man's got to obey the law." He held out his hand. "Give me your gun, cowboy."

Then a woman's voice rose above the muttering: "Hold on, Sheriff. I saw it all. The only thing this man did was ride into town. He didn't break any of your laws."

Everyone turned to look at the woman speaking from the buckboard. The sheriff's face turned crimson as he said, "Now, Miss Alexander, this is men's business. You shouldn't be worrying yourself over it."

"The law is everyone's business, Sheriff. Don't you think so?" Her words were sharp and crisp.

Adams coughed to clear his throat, and threw a hasty glance at Perkins, who spoke up: "All right, Carrie, you've had your say. Why don't you be a good girl and—"

"Don't Carrie me, Williford Perkins!" she snapped. "There isn't one of us here who doesn't know what's going on. A man comes into town and refuses to buckle under to your golden-haired deputy, and all of a sudden he becomes an outlaw."

"That ain't it at all, Miss Alexander," the sheriff replied. Pointing to me, he added, "He ain't got no job. He's a vagrant, and vagrancy is against the law."

Before I could answer, Carrie Alexander stuck out her jaw and looked squarely at me. "He's got a job now. I'm offering him one. How about it, cowboy? Do you want to work for me or end up in his jail?"

As everyone stared at me, I suddenly had the distinct feeling that I was a pawn in a much larger game of chess than met the eye. However, I didn't waste any time in giving her an answer, for considering the alternative to her offer, I didn't see where I had much choice. Besides, I was running low on funds. Cowboying didn't pay much, but twenty-five or thirty dollars a month with found adds up over a few months.

"Well?" Carrie Alexander was growing impatient. I nodded. "I'd be much obliged, ma'am."

Her eyes flicked triumphantly from me to Sheriff

Adams to Williford Perkins before coming back to me. "Good." She pointed to the road heading east out of town and said to me in a clipped, flat voice, "Two miles out, the road forks at the bridge. Take the south fork and follow the creek. My place is five miles down where the creek makes a large curve. The brand's on the sign, the Flying A. Tell C. H. George I said to put you to work." Without waiting for an answer, she sat down on the wagon seat, spoke sharply to the driver, and they drove on down the dusty street.

Sheriff Adams and the rest of the crowd had their eyes on the buckboard. I couldn't see any good in my hanging around Sweetwater Creek, so I pushed through the crowd and headed across the street to my buckskin.

"Hey, cowboy."

I stopped in the middle of the street and looked back. "What is it, Sheriff?"

"What's your name?"

"Shad Colter."

"All right, Colter. You got lucky this time, but don't you ever give me any reason to cross horns with you. You come into my town, you keep your nose clean, you hear?"

I kept my mouth shut and nodded. A look of surprise flashed across Williford Perkins's face. Quickly the man erased the expression, but not before I saw it.

Chapter Two

I found the fork with no trouble. The southbound road ran alongside the west bank of the creek, which was a pristine stream, clear and inviting, about twenty feet wide. A grove of cottonwoods lined the east side of the stream for a mile or so down below the fork.

I rode into the shadowy grove, and since I'd missed my beer back in town, I didn't waste any time sticking my head in the creek. The water was cool and sweet, reminding me of the icy streams high in the blue mountains of New Mexico and Arizona. Overhead, the breeze murmured through the treetops.

I rested on my elbows and stared at my reflection in the clear water, and for a fleeting moment I saw a dark-skinned face with laughing black eyes and a bright smile right alongside my own. I blinked my eyes and looked again. Her image faded into the sandy bed beneath the clear water. I closed my eyes and dropped my head. The bubbling water brushed my forehead for several minutes as I fought back the hurt that burst fresh inside me once more. Would I ever again find what I had lost?

Afterward, I moved deep into the cool shade of the cottonwoods and loosened the buckskin's cinch and ground-reined her to browse. Then I pulled a worn copy of *Walden* and a strip of jerky out of my saddlebags. Reading was one of the few good habits I had picked up from old Ned. I had read this book twice, but I never tired of Thoreau's observations of man's life and his values, observations as fitting in this generation as in the one when he wrote the book.

Before sitting down to read, I studied the country around me, another habit I had picked up early from old Ned, and one that had been honed sharp when I lived up in the Mogollons with the White Mountain Apaches, or *Tinnehs* as they once called themselves.

Apichi, meaning enemy, was the name given them by their earliest foes. The white man changed the spelling, and over the years, even the venerable old men of the tribes forgot *Tinnehs* and thought of themselves only as Apaches.

I tried not to think about the Apaches any longer, but that was impossible, for many of their habits and beliefs had become ingrained within my own nature. Like them, I analyzed the country around me as naturally as I took a drink of water or swallowed a bite of food. I automatically studied, cataloged, and filed any geographical feature I could use to shield me from unfriendly eyes.

Sweetwater Creek itself was in the middle of a broad valley that appeared to be twenty or so miles wide and infinite in length. On the flood plains stretching four or five miles on either side of the creek, bluestem and grama grass grew lush and thick. On the rising slopes beyond the luxuriant pasturage began the sagebrush and shortgrass prairie, dotted with sand hills that rolled across the prairie to the rim of the valley.

I was somewhat familiar with the geography of the Texas Panhandle, and from what Carrie Alexander had said about the creek's making a big curve at her place, I figured this creek probably fed into the Red River somewhere back to the southeast.

Suddenly, the drift of voices reached my ears. My buckskin looked up, ears pricked forward. Moments later two cowpokes pushing several cows came into view through the cottonwoods. About two hundred yards out on the prairie, they were moving due north and parallel to the creek.

Unseen, I watched from the shadows of the grove as the two passed, each throwing glances over his shoulder more often than seemed natural for someone with nothing on his mind. One rode an Appaloosa, a breed I seldom saw this far south. Most of those animals were with the Nez Percé up north. The animal made a fine picture, about sixteen hands, prancing sideways, his neck arched, his ears perked forward. The other cowboy rode a roan, a typical ranch horse.

Sometime later, while the trees blocked them from my sight and me from theirs, I snugged up the cinch on the buckskin and headed on down the road.

No one could ever claim he rode past the Flying A because he didn't see the sign. Nailed to the top of cottonwood poles, which towered fifteen feet over my head, a sign the size of a Conestoga sideboard faced the road. Burned deep in the middle of the sign was the brand, a large *A* square in the middle of an oversized *V*.

C. H. George was a wiry, bandy-legged man with a knot of tobacco stuck in his cheek. His wrinkled skin was the color of old leather, a common condition brought on by the relentless Texas sun, and the wrinkles in his face were as deep and abundant as the gullies and arroyos in the Palo Duro Canyons. But his eyes held clear and steady while I introduced myself. He showed me to the bunkhouse and said, "Take your choice of bunks. We got plenty to spare."

Without replying, I tossed my gear on a bunk next to the wall where I could keep my eyes on the door. C.H. said nothing, but I saw him arch an eyebrow at my selection.

"How many hands working for Miss Alexander?" I asked.

"Six now, counting you. Two of us, me and Ed Boswell, our cook, been here longer'n bulls been buttin' heads. Worked my whole life for her daddy, I did. In fact, I come in here with Jimmy Alexander and helped him settle this here land back in the fifties. Ed come a couple of years later."

As C.H. hesitated, a frown flickered over his weathered face as if he had bitten into an unripe persimmon. I didn't think anything about it at the time, but the expression would later come back to answer one or two questions nagging at me. He went on: "Frank Ruffner, he's been with us since about two, three years back. Solid man. Figure he's got some kind of past, but he does good ranch work. Long as he does that, what he's done before ain't worth a hill of beans. I reckon you seen him. He drove Miss Carrie into town.''

He nodded at two unmade bunks. ''Them belong to a couple of kids out of Abilene I hired on here last week—Jim Farley and Bill whatever. I forget his last name.'' He laughed and led the way out of the bunk-house. ''Only thing I remember about either one of them jaspers is that fine animal Jim Farley rides. It's one of them Appaloosas—you know, the kind with the spots on the rump.''

''I've heard of them,'' I replied, figuring Farley to be the cowpoke I had seen pushing those beeves north through the pasture.

Outside, C.H. climbed up on the top rail of the corral and pointed to the ranch as he warmed to his subject. The main house was board and batten with a fresh coat of white paint, and a covered porch stretched its full length. A spreading oak cast its shade over the hitching rail in front of the porch. ''Me and Jimmy planted that tree the second year we was on this place. It don't look thirty-five years old, but it is. I reckon its taproot goes clean to the middle of the earth.'' He paused and pointed at the lush grass on each side of the creek. ''A lot of possibilities here, Colter.''

He was right. The ranch had fresh water and belly-high grass that could fatten a steer overnight. The Texas weather was better for cattle-raising than any I had lived through up north. I listened as C.H. sang the praises of the ranch, but I heard more, not in what he said, but what went unsaid.

Possibilities remain only possibilities until someone takes some action, and I had the feeling that C.H. wanted to take some action to improve the ranch, but for some reason he was being held back.

"How many head you run?" I asked him.

"Twelve, thirteen hundred. Kinda hard to say for sure." He looked around at me and squirted a stream of tobacco in the dirt. "A place this size could handle five times that number and never graze a pasture more than a week." He clambered down and headed for the chuck house. "Come on. Ed always keeps the coffee hot. I'll get him to rustle you up some grub and build you a poke of supplies. Being the new man here, you might as well get the lay of the place by riding the rim. You see any Flying A stock out of the valley, push 'em back down. We got a late calf crop this year and I don't want to tempt any mavericker no more than necessary. Shouldn't take more'n a week or so. Line cabins ain't much, but after you run out the rattle-snakes, they'll keep the weather off you."

"Sounds fine," I replied, following the talkative and friendly little foreman into the chuck house.

He introduced me to Ed Boswell, the spread's greasy belly, a wiry little man with a gimpy left leg. Ed nodded and flashed a big, gap-toothed smile.

"Ed's the best cook in this state," C.H. said as he reached for two tin cups. "Ed, this here's Shad Colter. Goin' to be forking a horse for us."

"Howdy. Glad to have you with us." Ed pulled the three-gallon coffeepot off the stove and filled our cups with a steaming liquid so thick I could have walked on it. "Shad, huh? That's a right uncommon name."

"Reckon so. Full name is Shadrach, after the man in the Bible. The old man who raised me only read one book, and that was the one."

"Sounds like a right sensible jasper," Ed replied. "A lot of good sense comes from that book. I always reckoned that 'an eye for an eye' was as good a way to live as not." He set the pot back on the stove. "You any relation to John Colter?"

I shook my head. "Nope, but that's where I got the name. Ned Cooper, the old man who raised me, was pulled out of a sticky situation with the Blackfeet back in 1810 by Colter. The old mountain man by then had his fill of the West and headed back to St. Louis to finish his days. After I came to live with Ned, he gave me that name—kinda like a payback to Colter, I reckon."

C.H. spoke up: "From all I heard, it's a good name." He pulled out a pencil and piece of paper. "While you're drinkin' your coffee, Shad, I'll draw you a map of the place. Start you off up north, and you can make a complete swing around the ranch."

The week passed quickly. I discovered other valleys within the larger one, small bowls of a thousand or so acres filled with luxuriant grass and cold, sweet water. It was just the kind of country I could put roots into.

I worked hard and went to bed exhausted. That was the way I liked it. I didn't have time to think about what I had lost, to feel sorry for myself even though the hurt was four years old. I had left the mountains, and I was here to put it all behind and make a new life for myself.

The day before I was due to head back to the ranch, I swung down a gully choked and tangled with plum thickets and tumbleweeds, a perfect sanctuary for wild steers. Another arroyo cut off at a right angle, and so I decided to work up one side of that gully and back down the other, pushing any beeves I found ahead of me.

I came up empty, but just as I approached the main draw, voices cut through the silence. I backed my buckskin behind a wild-plum thicket in the side gully and waited.

Shortly, six beeves trotted across the intersection followed by two cowpokes, and one of them was riding the Appaloosa. Three of the cows were fresh, and each had a young calf tagging along. All three mama cows wore the Flying A brand.

Strange. C.H. knew I was up here pushing stock back down. It didn't make sense that, being short-handed, he would send two more men to do a job that was already being handled.

I considered what I had seen. In the back of my mind, a tiny suspicion burst into flame. But I would wait and watch, and keep my mouth shut.

The next morning I left the line cabin before sunup, planning to swing west to the canyons sketched on C.H.'s hand-drawn map. If I found any stock there, I would push them back to the ranch with me.

The canyons were wild and desolate. There was no

browse, but the sandy beds were filled with cattle sign, both old and new. I was puzzled. These canyons seemed to be too far from good graze for so many cattle to drift into them. The sandy beds also held tracks of snakes, coyotes, and other small animals. Once or twice I spotted the tiny hoofprints of antelopes. Soon I came to a fork in the main canyon. A smaller canyon cut off to the left, and from this offshoot, fresh horse tracks and cattle tracks emerged.

Curious, I backtracked the sign into the canyon. Around the first bend I pulled up. The canyon narrowed into a slender neck before opening up into a box canyon. On either side of the neck, two upright posts, with three evenly spaced blocks of wood between them, were lashed together and set in the sand. Three cottonwood poles lay on the ground, rails that could be inserted between the upright posts to serve as a gate across the box canyon.

I sat in my saddle and studied the layout. The only reason I could figure for a corral up here in these desolate canyons was if someone wanted to hide stock. And anyone hiding stock was up to no good. But as I rode back out of the canyon and up onto the rim of the valley, I told myself that I was the new man on the spread, and there was no sense in sticking my nose in something until I knew how it should smell.

Upon reaching the rim, I had another surprise. A red stake caught my attention, but I didn't think much of it until I stumbled across another one about a mile or so along the rim. I paused before cutting back toward the ranch. The afternoon was late, and the sun would be well down before I got back.

But my curiosity won out. I rode on, and sure enough, after another mile along the rim, I found a third stake. I had no idea what was going on, but I filed the information for later use as I urged the buckskin off the rim and down into the valley.

The ranch lay dark and silent, bathed in starlight. According to the Big Dipper, it was past midnight. I put up my buckskin and made my way to the bunkhouse, ready to crawl under my blankets.

The pulsing, orange glow of a cigarette in the porch shadows stopped me. A voice spoke. "Expected you earlier today." It was C.H.

"Swung through the canyons," I said as I stepped onto the porch. "Nothing there but rattlesnakes and coyotes."

"Yep. Nothing ever up there." The glow brightened. "You must've run a couple hundred head down. Ruffner, he said he spotted a passel of new ones on the south pasture."

"Sounds about right." For a moment I wanted to tell him about the corral and the cowpokes pushing the Flying A cattle north. But I thought better of it. Best wait and watch. Could be there was a logical explanation for the whole matter.

I pushed past C.H. into the bunkhouse. "See you in the morning," I said.

The next day was Sunday, a lazy day on most spreads. Breakfast came an hour later than usual. C.H. walked with me to the chuck house, where he introduced me around. Ed Boswell and Frank Ruffner were right pleasant jaspers, but the two younger hands, Jim Farley and Bill Hollier, just grunted and kept on putting themselves around the pancakes.

Frank looked at me as if he knew me. "Whereabouts you from, Colter, if you don't mind me asking."

The rich, sweet aroma of pancakes and honey reminded me of just how hungry I was. "All over," I told him. "Like they say, nowhere in particular and everyplace in general."

Jim washed his pancakes down with a slug of black coffee and dragged the back of his hand across his lips. "So old C.H. put you out on the line, huh? Must've been mighty exciting up there," he added, digging an elbow into Bill's side.

I laughed with them. "Busted my gut laughing myself to sleep every night."

C.H. spoke up: "Speaking of excitement, Jim, you ever run down that pack of coyotes what's been pulling down our stock?"

Jim tugged at his black leather vest and gave a sidelong glance at Bill. "We been lookin' mighty hard, C.H. Why, Bill and me have spent the last two days tracking them back south of here."

South? But I had seen them two days earlier up north. I sipped my coffee, letting my eyes play over the two cowpokes casually. Jim glanced at me with a smug sneer on his face.

"Yessir, C.H.," Bill chimed in, a broad grin on his freckled face. "We even got a shot at them once, but they was out of range.'' He rolled up a pancake and sopped up the last of the honey on his plate.

So far, I had kept my mouth closed, but these two were up to something, and it smelled a mighty lot like two-bit rustling to me.

Now, I couldn't find the right or proper words to give any kind of lecture on honor or ethics or any of those sort of ideas, but I've always worked for the brand. That's the way of it—that's the only way for a man to look himself in the eye when he shaves. He works for the brand. When a man pays me, he's got my loyalty, pure and simple. If I don't like the set of his jaw, I leave. ''Well, then,'' I said, setting my coffee down, ''there must be another jasper around here riding an Appaloosa.''

Jim frowned. ''What's that you say?''

''Just what I said. There must be someone else riding an Appaloosa.''

''Not on your say-so, mister. I ride the only one around here.'' He snorted and glanced around the table, as if to dare anyone to dispute his claim.

C.H. shook his head. ''Jim's right, Colter. No one else in the county has one.''

I pushed my tin cup away and scooted back from the table. ''You're right sure of that?''

By now, Jim and Bill were looking at each other. Neither quite understood the swing the conversation had taken. ''What are you driving at, Colter?'' C.H. asked.

''You been moving any stock around, C.H.?''

The two young cowpokes froze. Bill's pale face took on a shade of gray.

A perplexed frown wrinkled C.H.'s forehead. "None other than those you been driving down. Why? What's on your mind?"

I fastened my eyes on Jim. "Two days ago, on Friday, I spotted two cowpokes pushing six Flying A cattle through those canyons up north of here."

Bill shot Jim a frightened look. Jim's eyes went cold.

C.H. jumped to his feet. "You saw what?"

"That's right. Two riders were pushing Flying A cattle north, and one of them was riding an Appaloosa."

"That's a lie!" Jim shouted. He jumped back from the table and reached for his revolver.

I reacted instantly. In the next breath my .44 was in my hand, the muzzle trained on the bag of Bull Durham in Jim's vest pocket. He stiffened. The muzzle of his Colt had not even cleared leather.

Bill licked his lips. He kept glancing at Jim, then back at me, his eyes growing wilder and wilder.

The kid was on the verge of panic. "Don't try nothing dumb, son," I said, keeping my voice soft and calm so as not to frighten him into a foolish play. "You boys are in enough trouble now without digging the hole any deeper."

Jim tried to bluff his way out. "You're a liar, cowboy. No one is gonna believe you. Why, nobody even knows who you are."

Everyone in the room had their eyes on Jim except Frank Ruffner. I felt his eyes on me. But I didn't know why. "Has the ranch been selling off cattle lately?" I asked C.H.

"Nope."

Figuring Bill to be the weaker of the two men, I gestured at him with the muzzle of my revolver. "Why don't you ask this youngster here what the two of them did with the eight head they drove across the main road last week."

Bill spun to face his partner. "Jim—they know."

"Shut up, you dummy!" Jim snarled.

Bill cracked. His hand streaked for his gun. "I ain't goin' to jail."

"Hollier! Don't!" But Bill ignored C.H., and he cleared leather.

Jim seized the moment and went for his gun.

I fired.

When the smoke cleared, Bill lay on the floor, clutching his forearm, tears rolling down his cheeks. He was splattered with blood, but he was alive. Jim's right arm dangled limply at his side, but he, too, was alive.

I looked at C.H. "If you been losing stock, it sure hasn't been to coyotes, at least not the four-legged kind." I pointed the muzzle of my revolver at the two wounded men. "Considering the quality of the law you got in Sweetwater Creek, you'd be better off patching up these boys and hazing them out of the county unless you want to march them to the nearest tree."

Frank grinned but said nothing. C.H. nodded, then said, "We'll forget about the tree, but I reckon you do got a point there about the law.'' He jerked his head toward the cook. "Patch 'em up, Ed.''

A cantankerous old man, Ed Boswell shuffled forward, muttering. "I don't see why nobody else can't do the doctoring around here. Lord knows, being the local greasy belly for a passel of no-account cowboys and a spoiled woman don't give me a doctoring license. I ain't never been appreciated around here.''

I suppressed a grin and turned back to the two penny-ante rustlers. "Boys, you best figure you got off lucky. After you're patched up, you get out of the country. If I see either of you in the Panhandle again, I'll plant you three feet under the ground. You understand me?''

Bill managed to nod. "Y-yessir,'' he said, his eyes red from tears.

Jim just glared at me in a way that said he was going to cause me big trouble somewhere down the road.

Chapter Three

After Sunday dinner, at which Ed did himself right proud by whipping us up a dessert of hound ears and whirlups, crisp fried sourdough, and a water-and-sugar sauce with raisins, C.H. told me that our boss, Carrie Alexander, wanted me to come up to the ranch house. A big grin split his face. "Besides me, you're the first hand she's ever invited into the main house," he added. His grin turned sheepish, and he nodded at my denims. "I'd change were I you. She's mighty particular about her fancy furniture."

I was not really eager to visit Miss Alexander, but she was the one who paid my wages. If she wanted clean clothes on one of her hired hands before he came to see her, that was okay by me. "Well, I suppose I'd better make myself presentable," I replied.

After shucking my vest and shirt, I filled the tin wash pan with water. Though I had shaved before sunup, I shaved again and dressed in my go-to-meeting clothes. Nothing fancy, but they were clean. Frank Ruffner dug into his war bags and tossed me a bottle of lilac toilet water, which I declined because I was never one to care about smelling like a flower. When they insisted, I splashed a couple of squirts on my clothes.

Just before I left the bunkhouse, I strapped on my gun.

"Well, now," C.H. drawled, running his fingers through his thinning hair. "You look right purty."

Ed and Frank laughed with him. I joined in. It was a good feeling to be with friends, and I told them, "I hope it pleases Miss Alexander."

Dressed in a light-blue dress that swept from the floor to her neck, Carrie Alexander led me into the parlor. She was small, even what you could call dainty. Her hair was dark, and her skin the color of gold. She motioned for me to sit on a pink velvet couch. In front of the couch was a delicately carved coffee table with a silver teapot and a plate of sugar cookies.

She paused before sitting and glanced at the hat I was still wearing. "May I take your hat, please?"

She extended her hand, and cheeks burning, I tore it from my head and handed it to her. She glanced next at my clothes. I had been a few years without enjoying some of the simple amenities of a social life, so her invitation was right welcome even though her formality made a man a mite uncomfortable. She poured the tea and passed the plate of cookies.

"I want to thank you, Mr. Colter. You've saved the ranch some important money." She spoke to me as if she were talking to a tree stump, her words flat and without any feeling, completely different from the lilting warmth of Morning Flower's soft and gentle voice.

"Part of the job, ma'am. Besides, I'm the one who should be thanking you for speaking up for me back in town."

She permitted a small smile to play over her lips. The sun shone through her hair, giving it a trace of dark red as it outlined her heart-shaped face. Her voice was cool and reserved. "To be perfectly honest, Mr. Colter, I did it for myself just as much as for you."

I frowned but said nothing. She continued, her voice growing hard: "My father died last year. I came out here from San Francisco six months ago, and the entire town made it clear that they'd be just as happy if I went back. Seems like the whole place is against me, which makes me that much more determined."

As I listened to her, I began to understand just why she had taken my side back in town. She had spoken up for me to defy the sheriff and the town, not to help me. She went on to tell me how impossible it was to acquire adequate seed, clothes, supplies, stock, and even oil for the lanterns.

In the middle of her diatribe, as she hesitated and looked at me oddly, I could see her determination wavering, her resolve crumbling. Her cheeks colored and she stared at the dainty teacup in her lap. "I'm sorry, Mr. Colter, I didn't mean to get carried away. It's just that—" With her free hand she gestured to the walls around her. "Out here—" She searched for the words.

"It sure isn't San Francisco," I said.

Just as quickly as the shell about her had crumbled,

she resurrected it. "No, it isn't," she replied without emotion.

I knew how she felt. I had been an outsider much of my life, and I was still an outsider, but a man can't let that stop him. He has to work to become part of something. Even if he is welcomed, those who do so still must be shown he is worthy of their welcome.

"But Texas is a good country, Miss Alexander. Hard, unforgiving, but this country offers a man or a woman the chance to grow with it, to make a mark that will count for something in the years or even centuries to come. But doing so won't be easy. Nothing good, nothing worthwhile, comes easy." I nodded toward the front door. "Like that oak in your front yard. It had to struggle to survive this country, and to do that, it had to put down deep, tough roots, and enough of them to hold it tight against the worst that nature could throw at it. That tree will always be there." I sipped my cup of tea, then added, "And your being a woman will make it even harder in many ways to set your roots here."

Before she could reply, I continued, figuring I would say what I had to say, and if she decided to fire me, I could always move on. "You got to understand these folks too, Miss Alexander. They're used to dealing with men. Along comes a woman—a right attractive woman, if you don't mind me saying so—and people don't know how to deal with her. The womenfolk are jealous. The men are confused. Do they afford her the courtesy of being a woman and then let her take advantage of them on a cattle deal? Do they sell her the last of the seed because she's a woman?''

I set my empty cup on the table. "No, ma'am, they don't. I can see it isn't easy for you, but it isn't easy for them, either. San Francisco is city. Sweetwater Creek is country. These folks hereabouts don't cotton to city folks who come in thinking they're better than anyone else.'' She started to speak up, but I continued. "The way I see it is like this. If you understand just how hard it is on the townsfolk, you can use that to your advantage.''

"My advantage?'' She looked at me curiously.

"That's right, Miss Alexander, to your advantage. Dealing with a woman is hard for most of them, especially a city woman like you. If you make it easier for them, they'll be so grateful that they'll probably give in more than they normally would.''

A frown knit her forehead. "I don't understand what you're trying to tell me, Mr. Colter.''

"Don't be a helpless female. Out here, it doesn't work. Be more independent. The other day in town, Frank Ruffner was driving you in the buckboard.''

She nodded. "So? I don't know how to drive. Besides, back in San Francisco—''

I interrupted her. "Forget what you did in San Francisco. Sweetwater Creek is just about as far from San Francisco as China—at least, in the way people think and the way they act. Learn to drive a buckboard. That way you free up a hand for ranch work. Put on some pants and learn to saddle your own horse and get out and see what goes on with the ranch. Meet the other ranchers and merchants more than halfway. Once folks hear about it, and they will, you'll see a mighty big change in them. Texas is a whole different world from San Francisco. The sooner you learn, the better off you'll be.''

Her eyes blazed. She was not used to people speaking so bluntly, but on the other hand, she was not foolish, and she recognized sound advice when she heard it. ''In other words,'' she replied, ''you're saying that just owning the place isn't enough. I've got to pull my own weight.''

I couldn't resist grinning. She might be green, and hardheaded, and hurt because of the cool attitudes in Sweetwater Creek, but she was right smart. I told her, ''If you'd built this spread up like your pa, owning it would be enough.''

''But I didn't. And you're saying I've got to prove to them I can do the job.''

''Not exactly do the job, but at least give it a good try. You can fail, but if they see you've done all you can without whining, they'll stand beside you from now till Gabriel blows his horn. And as for your being a woman,'' I added, ''the merchants will come closer to working a deal with you than another rancher.''

She remained silent for several long seconds. Finally, she arched an eyebrow and said, her tone still businesslike, her reserve still intact, ''You're quite a sly person, Mr. Colter.''

''The Apache taught me, Miss Alexander. A brave who has mastered deception and trickery is held in high esteem by the rest of his clan.''

She scooted forward in her chair. For only the second time of the evening did her voice contain feeling, this time curiosity. "You lived with the Apache?"

Her question hit me in the pit of my stomach. I didn't want to dredge up old memories so I just said, "Some."

She didn't pursue her question. "Well, I appreciate the advice about the townsfolk, Mr. Colter. I'll think about what you have said."

I grinned sheepishly. "I wish it could be some other way, Miss Alexander. Now, if we were all back in San Francisco. . . ."

She studied me a moment, and a grin played over her lips. It faded into seriousness. "But we aren't, are we, Mr. Colter?"

"Afraid not, ma'am. Afraid not."

Her face became more somber. "Those two cowboys. C.H. told me you shot them."

"They gave me no choice. Ed patched 'em up. Nothing busted. They'll hurt for a few days, but if they got any brains, they'll learn a lesson from this. There's some ranchers around here would just as soon dangle those two from a cottonwood."

She saw that my cup was empty. "More tea, Mr. Colter?"

"No, thanks."

"Then I think we should get to the real reason I asked you to come up here."

"Yes, ma'am," I replied, sitting forward on the couch.

"I want you to run the ranch for me, Mr. Colter. Be my foreman."

Her words came as a surprise. "You got a foreman, a right good one, Miss Alexander."

She frowned at me. When she replied, her voice was testy: "C.H. is getting old, useless. Why wasn't he the one who discovered the rustling?" She shook her head. "No, I want you to be my foreman, and that's final," she finished, her voice petulant.

Reminding myself that she was green, I held my temper. When I replied, my voice was soft and calm. "I got lucky, ma'am. I just happened to be at the wrong place for them and at the right time for us. It was nothing I did on purpose, and with all respect, you best hold on to C.H. if you can. He settled this country with your daddy, and that old man would die for this place. That kind of loyalty you can't buy."

My words seemed to jar her somewhat, for she dropped her eyes and fiddled with the lace handkerchief in her hands. For a moment, her reserve faltered. "It's—just . . . I feel so helpless."

I studied her a moment. In a way, I felt kind of sorry for her. "Look, ma'am, you just turn over those worries and fears to C.H. That's what you pay him for. He'll handle them. You do what I told you about yourself, and you'll handle the townsfolk."

She looked up at me. For the first time, I had the feeling she was seeking help. "You can't be sure."

"Of C.H.?" I nodded. "Yes, ma'am, I sure am. And I'm sure of you, if you've got the sand I've been told your pa had."

A knock at the door interrupted us. A flash of impatience wrinkled her forehead. Then she gave me a bright smile. "Please excuse me, Mr. Colter."

I nodded and glanced out the window as she went into the foyer of the house.

A few moments later, returning with Williford Perkins, she wore a smug expression on her face. "Mr. Colter, I'd like to formally introduce you to Mr. Williford Perkins, our local banker."

I rose and extended my hand. The complacent grin on Perkins's face froze, and his eyes turned to ice when he recognized me. But I'll give him this: he thought quickly. He maintained the smile and took my hand. "Mr. Colter. It's good to see you again. I'm pleased that things seem to be working out for you now that you are in the employ of Miss Alexander. This is a much better environment than when we first met."

His hand was cold, but his clasp was firm. For a moment, I forgot the slender man was the town banker. He didn't look like any banker I had ever known. He measured me with the impassive, almost detached gaze with which one gunman eyes another.

"Thanks," was all I said.

For a few seconds the three of us stood about awkwardly until I excused myself. Leaving Perkins in the middle of the parlor, Carrie Alexander showed me to the door. "Thank you for a most informative visit, Mr. Colter. And would you please send C.H. up here?" She glanced over her shoulder. "I believe Mr. Perkins wants to talk business." She gave me a subtle smile. "I guess I need my foreman with me."

I nodded, surprised to find I was relieved that Perkins's purpose was business instead of social. Puzzling over my feelings, I headed back to the bunkhouse.

Later, when C.H. returned from the ranch house, he took me out to the corral. We stopped by the water trough. Propping a boot up on the trough, he said. "Thanks for what you said for me. You could've had my job for the asking. She's a tough woman."

"You're a good man, C.H. Besides, I'm satisfied with the job I got. If I had yours, I couldn't up and quit whenever the urge hit me. With mine, I can."

He rolled the wad of tobacco around his cheek. "That's what you say, but you don't strike me that way. You're a hard man to figure out, Colter. But you got a heap of good in you, I figure, especially after Frank remembered where he saw you."

Immediately, I grew wary.

C.H. continued in the matter-of-fact manner of a Western man who doesn't like to beat about the bush: "He said you saved his life up in the Rockies back four or five years or so. His party was hit by a band of Injuns—Apache, he guessed. He tried to escape, but a windfall pinned him to the ground. A large pine, he said. He couldn't budge it, but about then, a white man rode up, eyeballed him, and without breaking a sweat, lifted the pine and stuck him back in a hollow covered with plum thickets. Said you then pointed the redskins in the wrong direction."

His words brought back memories, both sweet and bitter. I didn't reply to C.H.'s unspoken question. Finally he asked it: "Is he right? You rode with the Apache?"

I studied the wiry foreman. He reminded me of a banty rooster, tough, unyielding, but conscience-bound to take care of his own. Yep, I figured C. H. George was one to ride the river with.

"Up till about four years ago," I told him, "I didn't ride with them the way you mean, but I did live with them. White Mountain Apache, they were, and I married one of their tribe, a little Indian maiden named Morning Flower. I was about twenty, she was sixteen or so. Apache custom is that the man becomes a member of the tribe into which he marries."

For a moment my thoughts drifted back to those glorious, carefree days. The two of us were so much alike. How I yearned for those days. How I hoped to find them once again—as she would want me to, and I her, had I left this world first.

We had discussed the subject, among many others, during our honeymoon on the banks of a bubbling little stream in the mountains. As we lay in the wickiup she had built for us from the skin of an albino buffalo, we both promised we would carry on with our lives even if the other could not.

"Dadgun," C.B. said softly. "How'd you get mixed up with them? I always heard the Apache'd kill a white man faster'n a dog could scratch a flea."

"Usually, that's what happens, but I saved one of their braves from a grizzly. He was the son of the chief. Best introduction I could have had. They took me in. I was young, footloose. And since I had nothing better to do, I took 'em up on their invitation to live a spell with them.'' I grinned as I remembered my days with the Apache. ''Lived with them five or six years, and it wasn't a bad life. That is, until—''

I paused, realizing I'd revealed more about my past in the last few seconds than I had in the last four years. But I figured I'd said enough. A man has to live through the experience to understand the Indian. You can't explain their customs to an outsider, and as good a man as C.H. was, he was a white man and an outsider to the Indian way of life.

He glanced at the .44 on my hip. ''You're mighty fast with that hogleg. Frank says he's never seen anyone faster, except maybe for Doc Slater.''

Everyone had heard much of the fast-gun Doc Slater, but he had dropped out of sight a few years back. Probably gunned down and forgotten.

''I'm not that fast,'' I said, hoping to discourage any more conversation in that vein.

''I heard he was a real live doctor at one time. He must've been mighty smart to be a sawbones.''

Deliberately, I nodded to the ranch house. ''You find out what Williford Perkins wanted?''

A look of disgust darkened his face. ''He made Miss Carrie another offer on her place. Can you figure it? He really expected she would sell this place her daddy and me built from the ground up.''

''So she turned him down, huh?''

''You're dadburned tootin' she did, and if she hadn't, I would have turned her over my knee and spanked her just like the spoiled brat she is.''

I had the feeling that something had been left out. "What made him think she would sell to begin with?"

The belligerence fled his face. He looked at the ground and scuffed up the dirt with the toe of his boot. "Well, she has a mortgage payment due purty soon. Perkins owns the bank."

"I see. So either he'll get it now or he'll get it later if she doesn't make the note?"

"That's about the size of it."

"Can she make the note? Does she have the money?"

C.H. shook his head. "This here place has always been cow poor. We'd sell off a few head whenever we needed cash. The merchants in town went along with us, but Williford Perkins came to town about three or four years back and started buying up everything in sight. He wouldn't let folks get by on credit no more. Claimed it was bad for his business. Them what owed him either paid up or he foreclosed on them.

"Well," he went on, "old Jim Alexander owed a considerable sum of money, and he did his durnedest to keep up the note. We worked around the clock, it seemed like. Jim fought a good battle, but he was getting up there in years, and the fight finally broke him. He passed on about a year back. I kinda looked after things till Miss Carrie got out here." He arched a bushy eyebrow. "You can tell, she ain't much of a Western woman."

I glanced up at the ranch house. "Maybe not yet, C.H., but give her time. I think she's got grit. Her problem is that she doesn't know how to get along with people out here, and she's afraid to take the chance to get to know them.''

"I don't know if she's got grit or not. Even if she does, grit ain't going to pay no mortgage notes.''

"Reckon you're right, but you got cattle. Round 'em up and sell 'em off.''

He shook his head. "We'd have to move seven, eight hundred. No market around here for that many.''

The number surprised me. "She owes that much?''

C.H. nodded.

"Take 'em to Dodge City. You could get more at Abilene, but Dodge is closer.''

He stared at me for several seconds, his mouth open in surprise. "Dodge City? You're crazy. I ain't never been on no cattle drive.''

"Not much to it,'' I said. "Not a whole lot different from pushing them around these pastures.''

"You've done it? Been on drives, I mean.''

"Some. The best bet would be to drive to the Western Trail, hope to hit it below Dodge City.''

"Western Trail? I never heard of it.''

"It's east of here right on the edge of Indian Territory. It runs about a hundred miles this side of the Chisholm.''

He shook his head. "Impossible. We ain't got the hands.''

"Hire more. You got to hire a couple, anyway.''

My suggestion had C.H. stirred up. He stared off into space thoughtfully. Finally he looked back at me. "What if we don't make it?''

"You're going to lose the ranch, anyway.''

He drew in a deep breath and looked me square in the eye. "You git right to the point, don't you? Well, Perkins might get this ranch, but it won't be because we didn't put up one ring-tailed, son-of-a-gun of a fight." He pivoted and headed for the ranch house. "I'm going to see Miss Carrie."

I watched him as he grew smaller in the distance. Old Ned Cooper had used the Bible to teach me to read, and over the years, I read every book I could put my hands on, figuring some of them would explain some of the hundreds of unanswered questions running through my head. In one, I read about the unusual and sinister tortures of the Orientals, but I didn't believe that even the most diabolical Oriental mind could come up with a torture worse than pushing eight hundred head of wild and contrary bovines from the Texas Panhandle to Kansas in the middle of the summer.

My buckskin stuck his head over the top rail and nuzzled my shoulder. Out of habit, I reached for the pump handle and began filling the trough for the thirsty animal. I sure wished that the other problems around here could be solved as easily.

Chapter Four

The idea of a cattle drive excited Carrie Alexander. She kept C.H. and me up in her parlor until after midnight, asking all sorts of questions. I pointed out every possible problem a drive would face, beginning with her lack of money to hire hands and purchase supplies. Then she would have to pull the herd together, point 'em north, fight off the weather, rivers, Indians, comancheros, and any rancher who didn't want her crossing his spread.

"And if the drive fails, you'll lose everything," I finished, wanting her to fully understand the importance of her decision.

She looked at C.H. "You were with my father for a long time, weren't you?" Her voice was still devoid of emotion.

He nodded, the lamplight reflecting off his balding head. "Over fifty years, Miss Carrie. We grew up together in Tennessee."

Carrie Alexander looked at me. A tear sparkled in her eye, but she quickly wiped it away. "My mother was from a socially prominent family in San Francisco. She left my father soon after they were married. She

41

detested this country and the people. Then her family lost its money. I never knew my father, but he sent funds to us regularly.''

An awkward silence filled the room. C.H. broke it. ''Your mama, she was a fine lady, but this country was too hard on her. Your pa was a good man. He knowed a family man had to take care of his own even if they was far away, and he done it.'' The old foreman shook his head sadly. ''Yep, he was a good man.''

Carrie Alexander studied C.H. for several seconds. A warm smile lit her face, and she leaned forward and laid her hand on the back of his gnarled fist. ''He would have to be to have you as a friend.''

Her move surprised me.

C.H. beamed.

She continued, her jaw set, her eyes clear, her tone matter-of-fact: ''I truly believe this cattle drive is what my father would have done, Mr. Colter. He spent his life building a name for himself, and I will do nothing to tarnish it.''

Leaning back in my chair, I nodded. She had made her decision. Whether it was the correct one remained to be seen. Such a drive faced tremendous risks, but, then, the men and women who built this country had faced such risks daily.

And she faced many hazards. But the one that most concerned me was C. H. George. No question at all, he was straight and honest, but could he be the kind of range boss to get the herd to market? In addition to being as mean as a panther, a range boss had to be half wise man and half crazy man. He had to drive men, push beeves, fight Indians, ford rivers, and charm cattle buyers. A huge job for any man. Could C.H. handle it? I didn't know, but I knew that all I could do was wait and see, and be there if he needed a hand.

"So," I said to her. "You're taking them to Dodge City."

She hesitated, swallowed hard, and set her jaw. "To Dodge City," she said.

Work began in earnest the next morning. Carrie Alexander had ignored my suggestion to learn to drive a buggy or wear pants. C.H. drove her, all dressed in pink calico and a large slat bonnet, around the county to visit the other ranchers within ten miles to tell them about the roundup. She paused only long enough in town to hire two cowpokes for the ranch.

None of the ranches were fenced, so when we started our roundup, we were bound to pick up stock from other owners. They could either send a rep to check our tally and drive their animals back home, or they could let us take their stock to market on commission. Two of the ranches, the Bar K and Circle Eight, chose to let us drive some of their stock to Dodge with our own.

The next several days were filled with the sounds of yipping cowboys and bawling calves, with the sight of thirty-foot lariats snaking through the air in every direction and frightened calves doing somersaults when they hit the end of the lariat, with the mingled smells of pungent sweat, acrid wood smoke, charred flesh, and burned hair. A thick haze of smoke and dust lay over the countryside.

Fifteen men worked, each on a different job that fit right in with each of the others. From the roper snagging the stock and calling the brands to the ironman tending the branding irons and to the extra flanker or swing rider immobilizing the animal, they all worked as one. After the calf was branded, a marker cropped its ear and tossed the sliver into a pail. Later, the bits of ears were used to double-check the tallyman. All male calves were castrated and given a cursory examination for ticks.

Above the hubbub of bellowing cows, yelping cowboys, and sizzling flesh came the rattling jingle of a steel bar against a triangle and the welcome cry of "Grub's on!" Work slowed for a short spell while a portion of the crew gathered around the chuck wagon to wolf down pinto beans, bacon, and fresh biscuits, all washed down with coffee strong enough to melt horseshoes.

C.H. rode up to where I was squatting on the wagon tongue and doing my best to put myself around Ed Boswell's noon grub while listening to the old cook bellyache about the work: "One of these days I'm going to get my own little spread and forgit all about these yahoos around here like they done forgot about me."

C.H. listened until Ed finished and stomped back to the kettle of beans. Then he grinned at me and said, "Looks like Ed's been on a tear again."

I shook my head. "Second time today." I swallowed a gulp of coffee. "Seems like he's gettin' to be a mite unhappy around here."

"Naw, that's just Ed." C.H. laughed. "He always gripes, though I got to admit he's done a heap more of it since Jimmy passed on."

I didn't pay his words much attention. "How do things look?" I asked, spooning up the last of the beans.

"Going good." He turned in his saddle to look at the stock grazing peacefully in the lush pasture in the curve of the creek. "New men seem to be working out okay?"

"Looks that way," I replied, referring to Peewee Stuart and Bob Cook, the two waddies C.H. had hired to replace our green rustlers. I had not worked with either man, but whenever I saw them, they were working, and they seemed to know what cattle were all about. Cook, the larger of the two, stuck by himself, but Peewee, who barely topped five feet, clung to other cowpokes like a homesick tick.

C.H. grunted. "Good. I hoped they would. Peewee worked for the Circle Eight before pulling up last year. He just got back in town. I knew he would work out. Cook was the one I wondered about. He's new in town."

"Well, Cook knows cattle and he works hard. You got nothing to worry about on that score."

To the north, a small herd of cows pushed over the horizon in a boil of dust. "That must be Frank and his bunch bringing them down from the canyons."

Off to the west, another plume of dust arose behind the rolling hills. "Appears someone's heading out to the ranch," I said.

C.H. scratched his head. "Wonder who it could be this time of day."

Behind me, wrapped in his blankets under the chuck wagon, the nighthawk groaned. "I don't give a rip who it might be. I just wanta git some sleep."

C.H. grinned at me, and we moved off to let the boy sleep. He would have his hands full riding herd tonight, so he deserved his rest during the day.

I slept at the wagon each night, but C.H. always reported in to Miss Alexander. The next morning he told me that Williford Perkins had paid her a visit the day before at noon. He made her another offer for the ranch, but she refused.

"Good," I said.

"She's worried, though."

I studied C.H. He was worried too. "Why?"

"She said Perkins warned her."

"Warned?"

"Well, maybe not warned, but he told her that a lot could happen on a cattle drive." He hesitated a moment. "She got the feeling he was trying to tell her we could have trouble—bad trouble—on this drive."

"Any time you mess with those hardhead creatures called cows, C.H., you're asking for trouble." I laughed, but behind the laughter I wondered at the banker's words.

C.H. coughed and glanced around. "I'd like to ask you a favor, Colter. You seem like the kind of man to ride the river with."

"What is it?"

"Well, it's like this. I'm getting up there in years.

This ranch is all I've ever known. Me and Jim held on to it against drought an' Injuns an' one kind of trouble after another. I don't plan on nothing happening to me on the drive, but you know how unpredictable them things can be.''

I nodded, and he continued. "If something does cut me short, I'd like for you to see it through for me." He dipped his head toward the ranch house. "Miss Carrie has a lot to learn. She can be right meddlesome and disagreeable, but she's old Jim's offspring and I'd sooner be dead than not do all I could for her and Jim." He gave me a weak grin and arched his eyebrows as if to say, *Well?*

I laid my hand on his shoulder and answered before I thought. "Be happy to, C.H. Be happy to."

The days passed quickly. Once or twice rain showers rolled through, cooling us off but never slowing the work. Closer to the ranch house, wranglers were busy smoothing out some of the greener broncos. C.H. wanted six to eight head of working stock for every man.

Within two weeks the entire job was done—cattle branded, horses busted, and supplies loaded. Reps pushed herds back to the home spread, chuck wagons clattered to the four winds, and old pals said their good-byes until the next roundup in the spring. C.H. and I stood on the hill overlooking the entire sight as well as sixteen hundred head of cattle, twelve hundred of which we would push to Kansas, and nine hundred of them were Flying A stock.

The afternoon sun was hot on the back of our necks. "Well," he said, "I never figured we'd get this far, but now, darned if I don't think we're gonna make it. And we're gonna have three hundred head of prime breeding stock left."

"You're right. Dodge isn't more than a couple hundred miles. I figure thirty days with luck." Glancing over the grazing herd we'd cut out for market, I said, "You built a good herd. With a short drive like we got, they shouldn't lose too much fat."

C.H. grinned like the proverbial possum. Maybe he had never been on a drive, but he knew cattle and he knew men. He had done a right smart job putting the roundup together. "Yep. They're all sound and oughta make Dodge City in good shape. From what I've been hearing, graze is good between here and there." He pulled out a plug of tobacco.

"You got your crew lined up? With twelve hundred beeves, we'll need ten, maybe twelve men."

"Think so," he answered while tearing off a chaw from the plug. "Counting you, me, and Frank, there's eleven going to Dodge. Ed on the chuck wagon makes an even dozen. I decided to leave Peewee and Bob Cook to take care of things here on the ranch."

"Oughta do it. Bob can catch up on his whittling."

"Yep. I never seen a man take a knife to a piece of wood like he does. Why, last night he took hold of an old white picket from the fence we tore down a few weeks ago. Says he's goin' to whittle a wooden chain." C.H. looked around. "Where are those two? I need to tell them they're staying before I forget it."

I hooked my thumb east. "Helping the Bar K rep push some of his stock home. You can tell them to-night."

He nodded and wheeled his horse around. "I'm rid-in' over to the Diamond Slash. You want to ride with me?"

"Nope. Got some gear to mend before we head out. I figure on nighting out here tonight, anyway. What's going on at the Slash?"

He patted his shirt pocket where he kept his tally book. "They didn't have a rep here. I want to see if they still want to send their stock to market with us." He touched his spurs to his animal and waved as he rode away.

I squinted against the sun as C.H. disappeared be-hind one of the sand hills. He was a good man, honest as the sun was bright, and as straight as the path from the bunkhouse to the outhouse. I might have wondered some at first if he could handle the drive, but now there was no question in my mind. C. H. George would get the herd to Dodge, and I'd be doing all I could to help him.

That night, Frank Ruffner shook me out of my sleep. "Colter! Quick!" he cried. "Somebody shot C.H. dead."

Chapter Five

We buried C.H. in the plot next to Jim Alexander's. Like Miss Alexander said during the eulogy, it was fitting that two old friends should spend eternity the same way they had stormed through life, side by side. Though I had known C.H. only a short time, I had the empty feeling inside that I had somehow been witness to the end of an era, a day ruled by rawhide-tough men who rode into a wild country and laid claim to a parcel, and with never a thought of failure, they fought rain and drought and plagues and Indians and even their own kind to make a place for themselves.

I looked at Carrie Alexander across the open grave. With C.H. by her side, she could have taken her time growing into Jim Alexander's shoes. But now, the luxury of time had vanished just as C.H.'s murderer had vanished.

She looked up and her eyes met mine. I forced a weak smile and she responded in kind. I wondered what C.H.'s death would do to the protective shell she kept around herself. I glanced at Ed Boswell. He stood there dry-eyed, staring at the grave. Once, I thought I saw a faint smile on his face, but I dismissed the notion immediately. Just my imagination.

The graveyard was less than a quarter of a mile from the ranch house. After the service Miss Alexander came up to me and in her clipped voice she said, "Let's walk back to the house. I need to talk."

I gave Peewee the reins to my buckskin and fell in beside her. I couldn't help comparing her to Morning Flower despite the pain my thoughts aroused. As she started to speak, her voice quavered and broke, but she didn't cry. She took two or three deep breaths, then said in a firm voice, "I didn't realize how much C.H. meant to me, or how much this ranch means to me. After you and I talked the other day, I did some serious soul-searching and, though I hate to admit it, the reason I came out here after my father died was for the money. We had lost ours back in San Francisco, mother had died, my uncle shot himself. I saw this as a chance to be *somebody* again."

"And now?" I asked.

Her eyes were red and puffy from crying, but her jaw was set and determined. "I think I understand what my father and C.H. and men like them died for. I can think of no better way to live than in pursuing the same dream they had."

I doubted she really understood the motives of her father and C.H., but at least she was making the effort. Before I could reply, she continued: "I need you, Shad. I've got to have a foreman I can trust."

This was the first time she had used my Christian name, and it surprised me. "Miss Carrie, I—"

She stopped and laid her small hand on mine. When she spoke, her voice quavered with emotion. "Please, Shad, I'm not being forward. I'm trying to be straight and honest. I'm trying to do as you suggested—to change and leave San Francisco behind. No feminine wiles. No deceptions." She paused, then added, "I need your help. I want you to take over C.H.'s job."

I had expected the request. But it was a job I didn't want and had not sought. In my years with the Apache, I learned much, but one of the most valuable lessons came from my deceased wife. She taught me that life is for the living. An old saw, and crusted with the hoary frost of a simpler time perhaps, but still fitting.

Now, I simply nodded, and together we continued toward the ranch house.

"When will you begin the drive?"

"Well, Miss Carrie, I—"

"Please, Shad. Just Carrie." I glanced down at her, and she was smiling up at me. "San Francisco is fifteen hundred miles west of here."

A warm feeling washed over me, like the time I first met Morning Flower. "I reckon you're right, Carrie. Well, I figure to push them out in the next couple days, but first I want to see what the sheriff found out about C.H."

Her eyes searched my face. "Be careful, Shad."

I forced a grin. A lump in my throat choked off my reply. All I could do was nod.

Sheriff Adams shook his head. "Not a thing, Colter. One of the ranch hands from the Slash found him alongside the road. His horse was grazing down the road apiece. That's it." He leaned back in his chair and hooked his thumbs in his vest.

I studied him closely. I had the distinct feeling our run-in on the street still rankled him, but if it did, he gave no indication of it. He kept his voice even and soft out of respect to C.H. And then, maybe I was just jumping to conclusions, I reminded myself.

"The slug struck at the base of his skull and came out at the bottom of his throat," Adams said. "No telling where the spent slug ended up, but I'd guess it was a .44."

I had inspected the wounds when we dressed C.H. for the funeral. The sheriff was right, and I'd guess also it was probably a .44 since almost every man and his brother in this part of Texas used that particular caliber. I nodded and rose. "Thanks, Sheriff. I appreciate the help."

He arched an eyebrow, then rose also. We both sensed the undercurrent between us, and both read several meanings into each word the other spoke. "Wish I knew more, Colter. By the way, does Miss Alexander still plan on making the cattle drive?"

"Yep. Next day or so, soon as we wind up some unfinished business."

"Unfinished business?"

"Ranch business, that's all," I replied, deliberately vague. But it wasn't all, and Sheriff Newt Adams knew it.

He shook his head. He was as curious as a kitten in a roomful of boxes, and he showed no better restraint.

"Folks figured Miss Alexander would think better of making the drive with C.H. dead."

"She still needs the money, Sheriff."

"Who's she got to ramrod the outfit?"

I grinned at him. "Me."

Leaving town, I headed east toward the Flying A, but once out of sight, I swung around and cut across the prairie to the Diamond Slash.

I had tried to figure out who would gain by C.H.'s death, and the only person I could come up with was Williford Perkins, the banker. He wanted Carrie's ranch, and if she didn't come up with the money to pay off the mortgage, he could foreclose on her spread.

But why? Why kill a man just for a ranch? Unless there was something on the ranch to make a man risk a hanging tree. But what could it be? I had ridden the entire spread. There were beautiful valleys, sweet water, lush meadows, but these could be found elsewhere. So what reason could there be for someone to murder C.H.?

The site of the murder was obvious. Grimly I sat in my saddle and stared down at the ground. Blood stained the hardpan. The surface of the road was like concrete, and the only other sign showing was the scar of horseshoes.

I discounted the idea of the killer riding alongside C.H. Whoever was behind the murder didn't want to take any chances. That meant ambush.

Keeping in mind the entrance and exit wounds on the body, I studied the surrounding countryside. The wounds indicated that the bushwhacker was on a higher elevation than C.H. The only spot on this wide-open prairie fitting that requirement was the crest of a nearby sand hill. With a cluck of my tongue, I turned the buckskin up the hill.

The sun was approaching its apex, and a suffocating heat radiated from the prairie. At the crest of the sand hill, I pulled up and looked around. The rising heat waves made the distant hills shimmy like the dress of one of those dancing girls at the carnival.

Sand does not hold good sign. The grains pour into the depression immediately, so all that remains is a vague trail that reveals only a general direction. I searched the area. Someone had passed the time here, someone who knew what he was doing. There were no cigarette butts, no empty cartridges, nothing to point an accusing finger in any direction, but I had the distinct feeling that this was where the killer had lain in wait.

I continued casting about, walking the buckskin in slow, lateral sweeps down the hill. Suddenly I pulled up and studied the sagebrush in front of me. Two limbs were broken, the result perhaps of tied reins being jerked loose. The ground indicated that at some recent period, the bush had been used to tie down a horse.

I shook my head in frustration. Suddenly, a shiny glimmer several yards down the slope caught my attention. Dismounting, I picked it up. It was a spur rowel, a five-pointed Mexican star with inch-long points, a wicked instrument that ruined many a good horse.

Slipping the rowel into my vest pocket, I scanned the area at my feet. Then I saw the heel prints. I couldn't help grinning at the irony of the situation. There were three heel prints, but right behind each print was a small hole punched in the sand, which had been dampened and firmed by the killer's horse. And the hole could be only one thing—the impression made by the very rowel I had in my pocket.

I looked up the hill and visualized the killer's actions after the shot. He had rushed down to his horse and yanked the tied reins loose, which accounted for the broken limbs on the bush. The sudden jerking on the bush startled his animal. The horse jittered backward as the rider attempted to mount.

I followed the vague trail around the base of the hill up to the road. But what had I accomplished? I was no closer to the killer's identity than when I rode out except I knew now that he wore Spanish spurs.

I headed back to the Flying A, pondering the numerous dead ends surrounding the murder.

As I rode through the gates of the Flying A, a hallo caused me to look around. Just outside a small copse of wild laurel on the far side of the creek was Peewee. He waved me over to him.

"What's up?" I asked as I stopped at the edge of the creek for my buckskin to drink.

"It's Bob Cook, Colter. He's got to talk to you."

"Talk? About what? Can't it wait until tonight?"

Quickly he explained. Cook had tried to draw his pay that morning. When Frank Ruffner questioned the cowpoke's sudden departure, the frightened man slipped up and admitted he had come to work on the

Flying A as a stooge for Williford Perkins to keep an eye on the roundup. "C.H.'s death shook him, and he's afraid he's next. Cook wants to talk to you and nobody else, so Frank locked Bob up in the bunkhouse with a guard outside the door."

I had no idea what was taking place, but a feeling of urgency caused me to dig my heels into the buckskin's flanks. The entire crew was waiting for Peewee and me when we rode up. "Where's Bob?" I asked.

Ed nodded to the bunkhouse. I dismounted and went inside. Bob had been pacing the floor. He stopped when I came in. He sighed with relief. "Am I glad to see you." He looked past me at the men standing in the doorway. "Just you," he said, his voice lowered. "No one else."

I motioned the men outside and closed the door. "Okay, Bob, now what's this all about?"

"I know who killed C.H."

His words hit me between the eyes with the force of a bullet. "You what?"

He shrugged. "Well, I don't know for sure who did it, but I know who ordered it. I think the killer was a Mexican brought in for that reason."

My fingers went to the rowel in my pocket. "Go on. Who ordered it?"

"The banker, Williford Perkins."

I caught my breath. "Are you sure?"

He hesitated. "Not one hundred percent, but I think so. He wants this place. I don't know why, but he does. From what I've heard, he figured killing C.H. would be enough to force the woman to sell."

I had been right. "What kind of proof do you have?"

He shook his head. "Just what I heard."

"We need something more than just your say-so."

"That's all I got."

"Did you hear Perkins order the killing itself?"

He looked around the empty bunkhouse fearfully. He gulped hard when he looked back at me. "Yes," he said, shaking his head. "I was in the back room waiting for him to see me, and I heard him tell someone to send for the Mex to get rid of C. H. George."

That was good enough for me. "All right. You stay here. I'm going for the sheriff. You give him your story and he'll put you into protective custody until after the trial."

Bob sat on a bunk and buried his face in his hands. "I wish I'd stayed back in Arizona. I was poor, but at least I could sleep good at night."

I ordered Peewee to stand guard outside the bunkhouse door with Frank. On the ride into town, I decided against telling Newt Adams about the rowel. I would just hold on to it myself.

Two hours later I rode up to the bunkhouse with the sheriff. Frank Ruffner rushed to meet us. "Bob Cook is dead!" he cried. "Somebody stabbed him!"

Chapter Six

Bob Cook was sprawled on the floor, his own knife in his back. Nearby, his empty supper dishes lay on the floor by the table. On top of the table was an empty tin cup lying on its side. Water from the cup had soaked into the tabletop.

"Anybody touch anything?" Sheriff Adams asked.

Ed shook his head. "Nope."

Frank interrupted. "I don't know if it's important, but when I found Bob, that picket he had been whittling on was lying across his legs." He pointed to a white picket on one of the bunks. "I tossed it on the bunk."

"What about Carrie?" I asked him. "Have you told her?"

"Yeah. After I found him, I called Ed and Peewee. I left Ed here, then went up and told Miss Carrie."

With a deep sigh of resignation, I shook my head. What else could go wrong?

While Sheriff Adams continued his questioning, I looked over the bunkhouse. All the windows were closed and locked. Frank and Peewee had been at the only door. The only man to see Bob Cook besides Frank and Peewee had been Ed Boswell, when he took

Bob his supper. I glanced at the empty pie tins that served as dishes. Bob must have eaten just after Ed left. And then someone killed him. But how did the killer get into the bunkhouse? More puzzling, though, was the question, How did he get *out* of the bunkhouse?

"Yeah," Frank said. "A few minutes after Ed left, Peewee and me heard a loud racket, and we looked inside to see what was going on. That's when I saw Bob lying there on the floor."

Finally the sheriff had questioned everyone, looked around, and ordered the body thrown over Cook's horse. As he started back to town, but not before, he made one last remark to me: "I reckon you know this drive of yours is probably the cause behind the deaths of these two men."

I saw through his poor attempt to rile me, and figured that two could play his game. "Well, then, Adams, maybe it's time for you to do some sheriffing."

His florid face darkened, and he slapped the reins against the horse's haunches with a loud pop. "Git!" he spat out.

Squinting against the setting sun, I stood in the middle of the road and watched Sheriff Adams until his dust had settled. But he was right. This cattle drive had stirred the pot. Two men had been killed, and I had the distinct feeling that the pot was still a far piece from boiling over.

After the sheriff left, I went back into the bunkhouse and looked around. Someone had placed the empty dishes back on the table. Bob had sure cleaned them up, I noticed. I picked up the cup and glanced at it. I frowned. There was a tiny hole in the bottom of the cup, one made by the point of a knife. That was strange.

The door creaked open and one of the new hires, Cal Stone, stuck his head inside. "Miss Alexander wants to see you, Colter."

Carrie was pacing the floor when I entered the parlor. Her face tight with strain, she said, "This isn't what I bargained for. You didn't tell me that two men would be killed because you wanted to take the cattle to Dodge City." I was at a loss for words. She continued: "You deliberately misled me."

The vehemence in her words knocked me back on my heels. "What—"

"Don't interrupt!" she snapped, jamming her fists on her hips. "You—"

"Hold it right there, lady! You got your facts a little twisted. You're the one who decided you wanted to take your herd to Dodge, not me."

She glared at me. "I wouldn't have if I'd known that two men would be killed because of it."

"That was a chance you took."

"I shouldn't have had to take that chance. You should have told me something like that could happen."

I shook my head. I was not going to stand there and argue with her. "Well, it happened, and nobody can change it. We got time to call it off. Is that what you want? Just say the word, or let someone else push your herd up there. I've got my craw full and I'd just as soon ride out of here. C.H. was wrong. Looks like you don't have your pa's grit after all.''

Her eyes blazed and her cheeks colored. ''We'll see about that. Go ahead. Take the herd to Dodge City. We'll settle this when you return.''

If I hadn't made that fool promise to C.H. during the roundup, I would have walked out on her right then. But I was stuck now. ''I'll take the herd to Dodge, but not because of you, Miss Alexander. I'm doing it for C.H. and your pa. You don't deserve the sweat off my brow.'' Without even a nod, I turned and left the house.

That night, Williford Perkins paid Carrie Alexander another visit. Had I known, I would have made a point of being within reach of her voice despite my anger with her. But the next morning, as I listened to her tell what took place, I figured that I couldn't have handled him any better.

Dressed in a pink cotton dress, she scooted around on the buckboard seat and faced me very calmly, giving no indication of the previous day's dispute between us. Frank was driving her.

''Williford tried to make me think he was only concerned about my welfare,'' she said. ''He offered me twenty thousand for this place.'' The fire spitting from her eyes matched the fire in her hair. There were sparks of anger in her voice instead of the cold ashes of boredom. ''He had the gall to call me a spoiled child. But I told him off.''

''Oh?''

"I told him I would never sell him the ranch. I told him I would burn it to the ground first."

I remained silent.

"He claims you don't have one chance in ten of reaching Dodge City," she announced, her eyes daring me to disagree.

I removed my hat and mopped my forehead with my neckerchief. I didn't have to prove anything to anyone. "We'll make it. Frank and Peewee are staying to look after things."

Without a word she scooted around on the seat. "Let's go," she said to Frank.

The next morning I rode into Sweetwater Creek and sent wires to the law in Dodge City, Wichita, and Caldwell, inquiring as to local troubles with Indians or raiders. I had no intention of using the railhead at Wichita or Caldwell, but I figured that if either of the towns had trouble brewing, it could spill over to Dodge. I plopped down in a cane-bottomed chair by the window to await my replies.

Outside, the traffic was busy for a Wednesday morning. Women in their sunbonnets and long dresses scurried in and out of the general store; men stood on the boardwalk in small groups, discussing everything from the weather to the accomplishments of U. S. Grant's second term of office. Buckboards, surreys, and wagons filled the street, raising a sheen of dust that settled in a gritty veneer over the town.

I received replies from Dodge City and Wichita within the hour. While I waited for Caldwell, I noticed a Mexican caballero in a wide sombrero riding down the street on a well-groomed roan. A *sarape saltillero* dangled across the pommel of the silver-inlaid saddle on which he rode. He pulled up at the saloon across the dusty street and dismounted.

I stiffened as he swung his leg over the roan's haunches. The rowel was missing from his spur. He pushed through the batwing doors as if he owned the place, an act curious to me, because Mexicans were considered only a step above a Comanche by most Texans.

Perhaps it was in his carriage, his demeanor; I could not put my finger on it, but this man did not give the impression of being foolish. Rather, he seemed to know exactly what he was doing.

At that moment the Caldwell wire came in. Without bothering to read it, I shoved it into my pocket and hurried to the saloon. I touched my fingers to my vest pocket, feeling the star-shaped rowel inside. Out of the corner of my eye, I saw Newt Adams standing in front of the jail and watching me. I ignored him.

The saloon was dark and cool. I paused just inside the doors to permit my eyes to adjust themselves to the shadows. The ripe, sweet odor of beer and the acrid smell of cigars filled the air, along with a low muttering of conversation throughout the spacious room. It was only ten o'clock in the morning, but the saloon was already doing a bustling business.

The vaquero was seated at a table by himself, a large mug of beer in front of him. His black eyes flicked up from the cornhusk cigarette he was rolling. They locked on me, then dismissed what they saw and returned to his task.

His dress was not that of the peon but of the *rico*. A caballero considered himself a gentlemen on a horse, and this one facing me was no exception. His sombrero was trimmed with a band of tinsel cord, his jacket was embroidered with gaudy braid and fancy barrel buttons, and his pantaloons, which opened on the outer part of the leg from hip to ankle, were set with filigreed buttons and trimmed with tinsel lace.

Under the table, black boots with silver toes stuck out from the pantaloons. He wore typical Mexican spurs, and on the spur nearer to me, a wicked star-shaped rowel glittered in the pale light from the door. The second was lost in the darkness under the table, but I had learned what I wanted to know.

With one hand I fished the rowel from my pocket and flipped it on the table. I slipped the rawhide loop from the hammer of my .44 with the other. The rowel struck with a clatter and bounced off the beer mug.

The caballero stiffened, and I said, "Here's the one you lost."

He stared at me. With a soft, greasy voice that belied his tightening muscles, he replied. "No, señor, it is not mine. I have lost nothing."

"You lie."

Leaping to his feet, he sent his chair tumbling backward. "I am no assassin," he cried. His hand flashed to the silver revolver on his hip. I moved faster. Before he could unleather his gun, I slammed my fist into his cheekbone. With my other hand, I ripped his revolver from his holster and threw it across the room.

He spun to his right, flailing his arms to maintain his balance. I followed him, and when he spun around, I hooked a wicked left from my waist into his jaw. His head snapped up and back, and he bounced off the wall.

His jaw must have been of rock, because he came off the wall with his fists lashing out.

I sidestepped and threw another left hook into his midsection. He caught me a glancing blow on the side of my head, but from the very beginning, I knew he was not experienced in fisticuffs. Few caballeros were.

Ducking my head, I bulled into him, driving my fists into his body like sledgehammers. He beat at my back weakly. Abruptly, I snapped the trunk of my body upright, sweeping my arms in an upward motion. Next I caught his arms and propelled them back over his head.

In the next instant we stared into each other's eyes. His were wide with pain and fear; mine, narrow with hate. He tried to bring his arms down to defend himself, but before he could twitch a muscle, I slammed a bony fist right between his eyes.

He sprawled to the floor. I stood over him, my chest heaving, my fists still knotted. After a few moments, he struggled to his hands and knees and managed to wobble to his feet, his fingers pressed against his face.

"Now, amigo, you're going to give me some answers."

He dropped one hand to the base of his throat.

The roar of a gun exploded in the saloon, and the back of the Mexican's head blew apart. The impact of the slug sent him staggering back, his eyes wide in disbelief.

Shucking my .44, I spun as I dropped to my knee and cocked the hammer.

Newt Adams stood in front of the batwing doors, his gun smoking. The florid-faced man looked down at me. "You were lucky I was here. He was going for his knife," he said, holstering his revolver.

Saloon patrons clustered around the dead man. A low muttering filled the room, but Newt Adams and I just stared at each other, my gaze accusing, his scornful. With a smirk, he nodded at me and left the saloon.

During my ride back to the ranch, I considered all that had happened within the last few weeks. The events reinforced the observation I had made that first day in Sweetwater Creek. I was caught in the middle of a struggle between Carrie Alexander and Williford Perkins. I had felt this was simply a chess game between the two. I believed it even more now, and I knew also that Sheriff Adams had sided with Williford Perkins.

And there was someone else, I reminded myself, remembering the killing of Bob Cook. Had the killer slipped in and committed the deed under our noses? Or was he someone on the ranch? There were four of us who could have murdered Cook.

The only new hand was Peewee. Frank Ruffner had been around for a few years. I couldn't believe he was the killer, for he and Peewee were guarding the door.

They could have done it together. They had every opportunity.

Then there was Ed Boswell, the cranky, cantankerous greasy belly. He'd been on the spread almost as long as C.H. What was it C.H. had said, that Ed showed up about two or three years after he and Jimmy Alexander settled here? It was his home, his life. Why would he want to see it destroyed? Yet he couldn't have killed Bob Cook.

Frank swore that Bob Cook was alive when Ed left after leaving a covered supper tray. He said he'd heard Cook drop some dishes inside. When he looked a few minutes later, the man was dead.

I went back over the events of that evening. In my mind's eye, I reconstructed the scene, from Cook's sprawled body to the empty tin cup on the table. Something nagged at me, but what? I had not overlooked a thing.

During my years with the Apache, I had learned that much of what appears obvious can be misleading. An empty prairie dotted with bunchgrass can suddenly sprout a dozen screaming warriors, or a log can abruptly burst into a fleeing brave. Is that what nagged at me? Had I assumed the obvious and ignored the true implication of something in the room?

I hung on to the problem like a pup worrying a bone. When the ranch house came into sight, I pushed my thoughts into the back of my mind, ready now to concentrate on my immediate problem, which was taking the herd to Dodge City.

I remembered the unread telegram in my pocket from

Caldwell. I uncrumpled the response and read it quickly. A tinge of concern welled up, but just as with my worries over the killings, I pushed it aside.

According to the wire, a band of renegades was operating around Caldwell. I pondered the information. Caldwell was a couple of days' ride from Dodge, probably too far off the trail to be too concerned about them, but not so far as to forget them.

Right now, my concerns were more immediate—weather and Indians. If the weather remained favorable and if the Indians stayed back east in Indian Territory, then we'd be okay.

And all this, I reminded myself, to help a spoiled, hardheaded woman who would probably fire me when I returned from Dodge City.

Chapter Seven

The next morning before dawn, eleven voices cried out, ten yipping at the twelve hundred head of cattle. The eleventh belonged to Ed Boswell, and he was too busy cursing his mules to worry about the cattle. He pushed out ahead, hoping to make five or six miles and then set up for noon.

I rode everywhere, constantly circling the lowing, shuffling animals, my eyes searching the horizon, happy to see only the stark, empty prairie before us. We had our hands full with the cattle. We didn't need any diversions.

The two men riding point that first day proved to be top-notch cowpokes. Cal Stone was one of them. The other was a young kid known just as Sawtooth, because three of his front teeth had been chipped in a brawl. "Whenever I smile," he had told me, "folks say I look like a crosscut saw."

I put them to searching for a bell cow, and within a couple of hours they had a rangy brindle steer with a horn span of almost eight feet leading the way. The remainder of the herd spread behind, three or four abreast, trailing slowly, pausing to tear up a mouthful of grass.

Two men rode swing, two rode flank, and two rode drag. One wrangler pushed the remuda. I rode wherever I was needed. For the most part, I was satisfied with the hands, but there were a couple I hoped I didn't ever have to put much faith or trust in. Still, they were good with cows.

Dinner that first day was black coffee and hot sourdough biscuits, after which Ed pushed on another five miles or so. That night the entire crew ate their fill of a mighty fine supper of sizzling steaks, gravel-free beans, hot biscuits, dried apple pudding, and, naturally, black coffee thick enough to walk on.

Quickly the crew fell into a solid, productive routine. Every morning around four they were driven from the arms of sleep by Ed's loud voice swearing that if they didn't hurry up, he would throw the bacon, beans, and biscuits in the creek.

Cowpokes struggled into their clothes, muscles sore and aching, some fighting off other aches and pains. They wet their faces from the spigot in the water barrel. Some shaved, and some, remembering their mother's admonitions, even combed their hair. Then they dried their faces with a community towel.

After the hasty breakfast, they selected their horses from a temporary corral that the wrangler had made with lariats. The next few minutes provided a top-notch rodeo that Easterners would have paid good money to see: lariats swishing through the air; horses working out their kinks with spins and twists and leaps, and bucking and sunfishing in a desperate effort to unseat the puny men on their backs.

Some mornings we permitted the cattle to graze as they drifted north. Other mornings we threw them on the trail before the sun peeked over the black line that was the horizon.

Ed moved out ahead of us, aiming for the noon break five or six miles up the trail. After dinner we made another five or six miles. And then we stopped for supper.

I made it a point to rotate the responsibilities, moving the men to different jobs. Drag was the job we all hated, and I spent my share of time back there.

In the middle of each afternoon, our nighthawk tossed his saddle into the wagon and turned his horse into the remuda. His job now was to grab forty winks, for he would spend the night with the herd. He had help from the crew, who worked in two-hour shifts throughout the night.

I rode up to the wagon as the nighthawk crawled over the seat and disappeared into the back. Ed nodded as he slapped the reins against the mules' haunches. "We're makin' good time," he said. "I figure about thirty-five miles in the last three days."

"That's what I figure. Ought to hit the Canadian tomorrow. Hope it doesn't slow us down. I'm riding out now to find a crossing. I'll see you in camp tonight."

"Take care," he said. "Most Injuns are back east of us, but you never can tell when a band of young braves might show up."

Ed was right about the Indians, but the ones to the east weren't the ones I was concerned about. The ones I worried about were those directly ahead of us, in that part of the Indian Territory just beyond the North Canadian River.

I rode ahead to the Canadian, a broad, silver band lazily winding its course across the vast Texas prairie. Cottonwoods and elms lined the river. I rode among the shadows of the giant trees, my eyes never stopping, always searching, looking for the unexpected.

A couple of miles to the west, I found a shallow crossing where the slow-moving, still waters broke into a chattering of ripples as they tumbled and twisted over and around the rock-strewn riverbed.

I tested the banks on either side. The sand and gravel were firm. On the rim of the valley on the far side of the river, I found Indian sign, but it was several days old. From my vantage point on the rim of the valley, I studied the crossing and the countryside around me.

The roar of the river faded into silence as my eyes swept the grandeur of the valley below me. The sky above was a brittle blue, and the air was still. The only sounds were of crickets and birds. But then I heard another sound, a sound that can be heard only on the prairie—the sound of vastness, of immeasurable space, a sound not everyone can hear. I looked down at the river. We would push the herd across before bedding them down. A river crossing is always chancy and I would sleep better knowing it was behind us.

The drive was progressing smoothly so far. I couldn't resist smiling to myself as I rode back to the herd. If things could just keep going as they were. . . . I spoke to my horse: "But that just isn't the way things go. Isn't that right, horse?"

The next evening we crossed the river without incident despite the grumbling about driving after dark. Several of the crew had wanted to wait and cross the next morning.

Around the campfire later that night, conversation turned to our good fortune so far on the drive and the possibilities of its continuing right on into Dodge City. One of the crew looked at me and asked, "What do you think, Mr. Colter? What are our chances of reaching Dodge without serious problems?"

Like most trail herders, the crew was young and full of vinegar, eager to test themselves against the most difficult and thankless jobs on God's earth. I shook my head and dumped my coffee grounds in the fire. "If I could tell you that, fella, I'd be making a living doing something else besides nursing cows."

Ed chimed in: "You boys keep on talking about all this good luck, and you're right certain goin' to turn it bad." He shook his head and stormed away. "Not me," he muttered. "I ain't going to be no Jonah to this drive."

Several broad grins greeted his warning, but they knew better than to say anything to Ed. They knew as well as anyone that a cook can get back at you in many different ways. The one jasper you don't want mad at you on a drive is the cook.

A gust of wind stirred the fire, filling the night with a spray of yellow and red sparks. One of the crew rose, banked the fire, and crawled into his bedroll. The others followed his lead.

I stood outside the firelight and studied the western sky. Bright stars twinkled that all was well. I hoped so, but I wondered.

The storm hit just after midnight.

I had been awake since ten with a nagging feeling that trouble was at hand. Ed joined me in the flickering light thrown by the small fire.

"Trouble?" he asked.

I shrugged. "Just a feeling, Ed. Go on back to bed. Three o'clock comes soon enough."

He grunted and fished a bag of Bull Durham from his vest pocket. "One of the good things about gettin' older is that a feller don't need as much sleep. Leastways, that's what I been noticing." By the time he finished speaking, he had deftly rolled a cigarette. He offered me the makings, but I declined them, never having picked up the habit.

Pulling a smoldering branch from the fire, he touched the winking red tip to his cigarette. The paper smoked, flamed slightly, then went out. For a moment the tiny flare had blinded me, but my eyes quickly adjusted to the darkness again.

Within an hour, a row of clouds rolled over the western horizon, their massive woolpacks lit by the white and yellow explosions of lightning. The storm was miles away, because the thunder was only a murmur, sometimes lost in the wind.

"That what you was worrying about?" I asked Ed.

His tone seemed casual, but his face reflected his concern. "That's it."

"Good thing we crossed the river." I nodded at the sleeping men. "Let's roust 'em out. We're going to be mighty busy in a few minutes."

And we were.

The wind picked up, blowing in dust from the prairie, stinging our eyes and clogging our nostrils. The great rolling clouds moved ominously toward us, their interiors lit with eerie glows in a cataclysmic display of yellows and whites and blues. The accompanying thunder grew louder, like the pounding of a million hooves in a wild and ghostly stampede across the heavens.

Had I been forced to select a site to weather the storm, I couldn't have found a better one than our present spot. We were down in a valley, bunched beside a windbreak of cottonwoods and elms, with the restless herd held on two sides by the curve of the river. If they ran, there were only two directions they could go.

Three of the men rode slowly through the herd, singing their ditties in a soft voice to calm the frightened animals. The other riders rode along the two sides facing the prairie. Ed had battened down the wagon and driven it under an overhang just beneath the rim of the valley.

"Easy, boys," I cautioned the men. "Last thing we need is a stampede."

Faces taut with tension, pale with fear, they nodded.

The gusting wind pelted us with splatters of rain. The time between lightning flash and thunder grew less.

With the wailing moan of a banshee, the storm howled into the valley just after midnight, carrying with it a veil of rain so heavy that even in the ghostly blue light cast off by the lightning, I could not see my buckskin's head before my eyes.

Like a giant string of firecrackers, one bolt of lightning after another exploded and crashed around us, lighting the valley with an eerie glow.

The herd was trying to run. The frightened animals pushed into the river, but the strong current forced them back. Several were caught up in the current, and bawling mournfully, were swept away by the quickly rising waters.

My ears echoed with the constant cracking explosions. I knew we couldn't hold the herd, and was surprised we'd held them as long as we had. The animals bawled, their wide eyes rolling with fear.

Suddenly, I felt a tingling sensation. Without hesitation, I threw myself from the saddle. In the next instant, a deafening explosion erupted next to me. Dazed, I lay on the ground, the rain beating down on my upturned face. Finally, I rolled over. Blazing flames leaped from the splintered trunk of a giant cottonwood. I struggled to my feet and looked around for my horse. The animal lay on the ground a few feet away.

I knelt and laid my hand on his neck. After a moment, he clambered to his feet. I swung into the saddle. Neither of us seemed injured, although my ears rang like church bells and I had to cling to the saddle horn to keep from falling until the dizzy spell passed.

But the herd held tight. A sense of pride swept over me. This was a great crew. They were managing to hold twelve hundred head in check in the midst of such a vicious electrical storm. They rode among the animals, trying to calm the jittery ones. Each knew how close the herd was to bolting, and each knew the danger of riding among the animals. If the herd broke with them in the middle, their horse was the only thing between them and certain death.

Slowly, the electrical storm moved past.

A young cowpoke rode by me just as the crash of lightning lit the countryside. He grinned, his rain-slick face a mask of weariness. Water poured off the brim of his hat onto his black slicker. "Looks like we held them, Mr. Colter," he said.

Before I could reply, his horse squealed and spun and reared, and then pawed at the roiling clouds with its front feet. And then a sharp pain struck me in the middle of my back, as if someone had hauled off and slammed a fist into my spine. Another blow struck my shoulder, followed by another on the nape of my neck. I snapped around, and a hard, cold object slammed into my jaw.

Hailstones!

From the surrounding darkness, horses squealed, cattle bawled, men shouted as the storm of hail pounded down on us. Suddenly, the herd broke, and as of one mind, they burst through the riders and raced north out of the valley, carrying with them everyone and everything in their path.

Ignoring the hailstones, I leaned over my buckskin's neck and raced with the cattle. The pounding of hooves, the rattling click of horns, the bawling of cattle filled the dark night. The heat of the cattle enveloped me as they jostled me and my buckskin.

I gave the buckskin his head, trusting him to find a way out of the stampeding herd. A range-smart horse, the buckskin slowly made his way to the edge of the herd, and by the time we reached the rim of the valley, the herd was on my right. Tightening my legs against the buckskin's ribs, I urged more speed from him.

He responded, although I could feel him flinch when a hailstone caromed off his nose or struck near his eyes. Behind me was a wild cacophony of sound, but piercing the roar of the herd was the yip of the cowboys as they struggled to keep pace with the herd.

Within minutes I reached the lead steer. Two other riders pulled up beside me. During a flash of lightning, I recognized Sawtooth, his ragged grin blazing like a lantern. For several seconds we raced shoulder to shoulder, finally passing out of the hailstorm. Then I began easing the buckskin into the lead steer, pushing the frightened animal into a large circle. The other cattle followed.

Together, Sawtooth and I continued pushing the lead animals into a circle until they slowly circled back into the herd and brought the stampede to an end.

Thunder from the fading storm echoed across the prairie. Overhead, the clouds pushed past, leaving behind an inverted bowl filled with bright stars. The cattle milled about, still on edge.

The remainder of the night we spent soothing the nervous animals by walking our horses among them and lullabying them in our thin, off-key voices. Just before sunrise, at false dawn, the mouth-watering smell of boiling coffee drifted to us from across the prairie.

In groups of three, we rushed back to the wagon to gulp down a hasty breakfast of biscuits, beans, and coffee, to throw our saddles on a fresh broomtail and hold on wearily while it bucked its kinks out, and to finally hightail it back to the herd. I waited until everyone was back before taking my turn.

The cattle remained restless. The only way to calm them was to throw them on the trail and let them work out their jitters, which is exactly what we did.

The Texas sun beat down without mercy, quickly drying the prairie. By the middle of the afternoon, sand and dust enveloped us like some kind of yellow fog, stinging our eyes, clogging our nostrils. We pushed ahead, unmindful of the discomfort, something we could tolerate as long as the animals remained calm.

A few uneventful but hot days later, we crossed the North Canadian and, after nighting at the river, struck out across Indian Territory to the Cimarron River, about four or five days to the north.

We all rode with every sense alert, expecting the unexpected. Although the Indians had been peaceful of late, even the slightest offense, intentional or not, could set them off.

"What do you think, Mr. Colter?" Cal Stone asked as we stared out over the empty prairie early one morning before hitting the trail. "Are they out there?"

I nodded grimly and pulled my hat down snug on my head. "They're out there," I told him.

Chapter Eight

The drive fell back into its routine. During the early morning, we moved slowly, giving the cattle time to graze, and then we pushed them hard on the trail, hoping to make five or six miles before noon. About midmorning, I rode on ahead to find a noontime pasture that other herds had not grazed or bedded. From time to time, I ran across the carcass of a buffalo picked clean by scavengers, its bones shining white in the sunshine.

The point men kept their eyes on me, because the only way I could direct them at a distance was by standing my horse broadside to the oncoming herd and pointing his head in the direction they were to move the herd. By the time the herd had settled in on the noon graze, Ed had the midday meal ready. As with every meal, we ate in two shifts, always keeping five or six men with the grazing herd. Then we pushed out for the afternoon drive, that portion of the day when the dust and heat and seared countryside emphasized the tedium of the drive. But there was not a man among us who did not prefer the everyday tedium to the stark terror of stampedes or Indian attacks.

The sun baked us. Dust choked us. Monotony bored us. The only sounds were the creak of saddle leather, the muffled crack-crack of the cows' ankle joints, the constant thud of cattle hooves, and the clack-clack of six-foot horns striking each other.

One day the tedium was shattered when a small band of six Kiowa appeared on the crest of a small hill. I pulled up and studied them. They weren't dressed for war, but I had seen as many battles between braves wearing no paint as I had between braves all painted up.

Cal Stone pulled up beside me. "They finally showed up," he said. "Think they'll jump us?"

"Maybe. Could be all they want is a steer."

The young cowboy gulped and forced a weak smile. "I'd sooner give 'em one than argue with 'em."

I grinned at him. "Me too, boy. Me too." With a cluck of my tongue, I urged the buckskin toward the Kiowas. "Come on, son, but keep your fingers away from that hogleg on your side."

Luck was with us, for the Kiowa had been sent by Two Hatchets for beef. I let them select six of the herd.

"A cheap price for letting us cross their land," I told Ed at supper that night.

"Waste of good beef," snarled one of the crew, a bewhiskered man who called himself Blackjack. Blackjack was one of the two I'd had some reservations about hiring. "Oughta shot them Injuns dead."

"That makes sense to me," said a cowboy by the name of Emmett Baldow. He was the second of the two I had pondered over hiring, and I had noticed that the two men had taken to hanging together around the chuck wagon in the evenings.

I shook my head at the two men. "And have a whole tribe down here on us? I'll settle for things staying quiet and peaceable."

We pushed on, crossing the Cimarron River several days later and moving on into Kansas, a state for almost fourteen years, but with its borders still ravaged by raiders. Nevertheless, each day put us closer to Dodge.

After leaving the Cimarron, we skirted Mount Jesus and headed for Bluff Creek, a tributary of the Arkansas River, which would put us about twenty miles from Dodge. From what I'd been told, the grass was good and the water sweet at Bluff Creek. A few days' good graze would put some lost fat back on the herd. In the meantime, I would ride into Dodge and set up a time for the buyers to take a look at the herd.

I left Ed in charge late that morning as I turned the buckskin toward Dodge. Three hours later, about two o'clock, I forded the Arkansas at a shallow crossing north of Dodge and rode into the city, only three years old but already a wild and exuberant magnet for whiskey-starved cowboys coming in off the trail.

Lining one side of Front Street was a row of board and batten buildings mixed with mud-chinked cabins and tents, tonsorial parlors for baths and shaves and haircuts, general stores for new clothing, a drugstore for those with a thirst for sweets, and saloons and dance halls for those with other kinds of thirst. On the other side of Front Street was the Atchison Topeka and Santa Fe tracks.

My first stop was the sheriff's office, but he was out. Over at Caldwell, the deputy said. So I headed for the Long Branch, where, over a cold beer, I met with three buyers who agreed to accompany me to the herd the next morning to bid, refusing my suggestion to ride out that afternoon.

"It'll be well after dark when we get back, Mr. Colter." The buyer laughed and added jovially, "And after dark is drinking time. Be a damned shame to waste all that valuable darkness on a horse."

The other buyers laughed with him and toasted his remarks.

"Besides," he added. "Tolbert is out looking at a herd now. He buys for a company out of Chicago, and he'd sure want to take a look at your stock also."

"Yep." One of the buyers winked at me. "John Tolbert is new out here. Came in last week. He still hasn't figured out what is more important—buying cows or drinking good bourbon."

I grinned and downed the last of my beer. "Okay, gents. You know where we are. I'll be expecting you in the morning."

Outside, I paused on the boardwalk and gazed at the setting sun. Long, wispy clouds stretched along the horizon, painted with brilliant oranges and rich purples. It was sort of like, I told myself, the Good Lord putting a proper end to a proper day.

And the day had been just that. We had reached our goal. The buyers were all primed, and I figured we could get ten dollars a head. After the hands were paid off and all bills settled, the Flying A would have about six thousand to take care of the bank note, with about a thousand left over.

I took a deep breath and stared across the Kansas prairie. Yeah, I was feeling pretty fit. And when I got back to Sweetwater Creek, I figured I would take another look at the valley through which the Canadian River flowed. The land was rich and the grass was thick. A good place to put down roots.

Off to the north, a handful of dots rose from the riverbank. I studied them casually, figuring them to be riders from another herd coming in for a go-around with Cyrus Noble whiskey and taking a whirl at bucking the tiger, a game of chance I had never mastered and was content to leave alone.

In the middle of the riders was a wagon, a large, lumbering chuck wagon. A chill ran up my spine. I drew my tongue across my suddenly dry lips and stuck my hand up to shade my eyes against the glare of the setting sun off to my right.

The riders were still only silhouettes, too distant for me to discern any features, but for the last several weeks, I had seen their silhouettes, knew how each buster sat his horse, heard the peculiar creaks and groans from Ed's wagon. They all appeared mighty familiar, and that was impossible. What would they be doing here in Dodge? Who was with the herd? What in tarnation had happened to the herd?

They must have spotted me on the boardwalk, because two of the riders in front spurred their horses into an all-out gallop toward me, waving their hats over their heads.

In two steps I swung onto the buckskin and yanked him around to meet them. The oncoming riders pulled up and looked back toward the chuck wagon. In the distance Ed stood up in the wagon and waved me to him.

Ed shouted at his mules and hauled back on the reins. His weathered face was flushed with anger. "Texas fever!" he shouted even before I reached him. "The cows got Texas fever."

"What?"

Ed nodded vigorously. "The sheriff from Dodge came in with a dozen or so deputies. Looked at the cows and claimed they had Texas fever. Said they had to be quarantined and shot."

The other wranglers crowded in around us as Ed continued. "He said they had to do the same to most of the Texas herds coming in. I told 'em to wait for you, but he said he didn't have the time. There was another herd back west he had to git to."

I shook my head. I was familiar with the disease and its carriers, ticks. I hadn't examined every head, but during roundup we looked for ticks when we threw the male calves, and we found very few, certainly not enough to warrant destroying the herd. Besides, Texas fever doesn't contaminate the meat of Texas cattle.

"Then what?" I looked around at the men accusingly. "What are you doing here?"

Ed spoke for them: "The sheriff made us leave. Told us to go on into Dodge City." He paused and shook his head. "Then they started shooting the cows."

"All of them?"

Ed shrugged. "Well, now, I can't rightly say. We had already left and was about a mile away when they started shooting."

A blinding rage exploded inside me. My ears roared, and I felt the blood coursing through my veins like a steer full of loco weed.

Sawtooth spoke up: "I hung back and saw 'em begin shooting into the herd, Mr. Colter."

I stared across the prairie.

"What you got in mind, Shad?" Ed asked.

Taking a deep breath, I tore my eyes from the southern horizon and looked at him. "I'm going to see me a sheriff. Somebody is going to pay for those beeves or I'll tear this whole country apart." I focused my eyes on Ed and fought to control the anger in my voice. "You might as well go on into town, Ed. No sense in pulling the wagon back out there."

He snorted and wheeled the four mules in a circle. "Bull. We're goin' to be needin' coffee, anyway."

I smiled grimly. "Okay. Let's go, boys."

Despite the encroaching darkness, not one man protested. I kicked the buckskin into a running walk, suppressing the urge to fly across the prairie. I know of only a few horses that could make a twenty-mile dash without killing themselves, and while this buckskin was a sound, dependable animal, he wasn't one of those few. Besides, the crew had already ridden twenty miles and their horses were tired.

There was no moon, but the stars illuminated the prairie with a bluish glow. I alternated our pace between a running walk and a walk in order to cover long distances without tiring the horse excessively. The first flush of anger cooled, replaced by a cold determination to get to the bottom of whatever was going on here.

I attempted to analyze the situation. Sure, I knew just as well as every other Texas cowpuncher what Texas fever could do to those animals not immune to it. So I had decided to avoid Kansas cattle. That was the main reason we had come to Dodge. Most of the domestic cattle in Kansas were over around Caldwell or Wichita and farther to the east, not at Dodge. As for humans, the fever didn't bother them—at least, in no ways that I had ever heard of.

So, to my way of thinking, if the herd was infected, the sheriff could have insisted we swing farther west, bypass Dodge, and head over to Pueblo or on up to Julesburg. Why hadn't he?

At the slower pace, we reached Bluff Springs just after one o'clock. I paused some distance away, expecting to see fires, but the prairie was dark. We spread out in a skirmish line and rode in with guns drawn. I squinted into the darkness, again not seeing what I had expected to see.

I had expected to see the carcasses of twelve hundred head of cattle, yet all I could make out in the darkness were only five.

Ed pulled up beside me in his wagon. "What the blazes is going on here, Shad?"

Holstering my gun, I shook my head. "That's what I'd like to ask you, Ed. You said they came up here and ran you off and then started shooting the cattle."

Some of the other riders had gathered around us.

Several nodded emphatically. "That's gospel, Mr. Colter," Cal Stone said. And another said, "I'll swear on a stack of Bibles, boss."

"Maybe the sheriff realized the cattle weren't sick after all," another crew member offered.

I stared onto the darkness surrounding us. Then where were the cattle and the sheriff? We met no one on our way back from Dodge. A tiny ember of suspicion burst into flame in my mind. If the sheriff realized he had made a mistake about the disease, he would simply have left a few men with the herd and come into Dodge to get us. But what if the entire plan had been an elaborate attempt to rustle the stock? Such an idea was bizarre, but I could think of no other.

Best I could figure, about seven hours had elapsed since the sheriff ran the crew into Dodge. Wherever the cattle were, they couldn't be more than five or six miles from us.

"Okay, boys, here's what we're going to do," I said.

I broke them into teams of two and scattered them in every direction except Dodge. "I figure we can run the herd down in a couple of hours. When you find them, one of you come back here to the wagon while the other cowpoke tags after the herd. Otherwise, we'll all meet back here around sunup."

I headed northeast by myself. Picking up sign at night was just about like trying to grab water with your fingers—next to impossible. There was sign that a herd had passed ahead of me only recently, but none of the cow patties were fresh enough to be ours.

After a couple of hours I turned back. When I reached the wagon, about half the crew was gathered around the fire, gulping Ed's coffee and sopping cold biscuits in hot molasses.

I shook my head as I dismounted. "Nothing out there. What about you boys?" I grabbed a tin cup and dipped a cupful out of the pot.

None of them had found anything.

"Then them boys back east oughta be stumbling over the herd," Ed muttered.

I looked toward the slowly graying horizon. "That's the way it appears."

Ten minutes later we had our answer. The two riders from the east came blistering in, their youthful faces a mixture of concern and suppressed excitement. Cal shook his head as he swung off his horse. "No herd," he cried, "but we found what happened to them."

Ed snorted. "Now, how the devil can you tell what happened to them if you didn't find them?"

The first young man didn't take his eyes off me. "There's a railroad spur about six miles east of here. We followed sign to the spur. Best we can figure, they drove the herd into the corrals and loaded them."

"There must've been a train waiting, Mr. Colter," Sawtooth said.

All my nagging questions now had their answers, except for one. I tossed the remainder of my coffee in the fire and flipped the cup to Ed. "You boys put everything together and come on in to Dodge." I swung into my saddle.

"Where you going?"

I looked down at Ed and unleathered my .44 and spun the cylinder. The action was smooth and slick. "I reckon the sheriff and me have got a small problem to settle." With a click of my tongue, I turned the buckskin toward Dodge City.

"There ain't that much to do here," Ed called out. And then I heard him shouting orders to the cowhands. Pots clanged, horses nickered, men muttered, and within five minutes the wagon and ten angry cowhands had pulled up beside me.

Dodge City lay straight ahead, unsuspecting of the fury raging inside the chest of eleven outraged Texans.

Chapter Nine

Curious men paused on the board-walk that stretched in front of the dreary facade of mud-chinked cabins and weatherworn board and batten stores to stare at us as our unlikely looking contingent rode into Dodge the next morning.

We headed straight for the sheriff's office, looking neither to the left nor to the right. By now, the rashness of hot anger had long disappeared. I had never been more cool or collected than I was when I dismounted and strode across the boardwalk. Behind me came ten grim and determined men.

I shoved the door open and stepped inside, every muscle taut. Three men were in the office, two by a stove on which sat a blackened coffeepot and the third behind the only desk in the office. Behind him was a rack of rifles. He looked up at me and smiled, but the smile quickly faded from his ruddy face when he saw the men behind me.

He leaned forward, both hands on the desk before him. When he spoke, his voice was soft but firm. "Hello, boys. Something I can do for you?"

"You the sheriff here in Dodge?" I asked.

93

He nodded. "That's right. Max Smith's the name."

Keeping my eyes on the sheriff, I spoke over my shoulder to Ed. "This the jasper?"

Ed stepped up beside me and peered at the sheriff, whose face colored. "Nope. This ain't the one."

"You the only sheriff in Dodge?"

His eyes darted at Ed, then back at me. "Yeah. Now do you mind telling me just what in blazes is going on?"

I forced my muscles to relax despite the fresh surge of frustration sweeping over me. "My name's Shad Colter, Sheriff. We came up from Texas with a herd of beef." I went on to tell him all that had happened. I noticed that when I told him about the railroad spur, he glanced at the two men by the stove. I didn't say anything about the look, but I filed it in the back of my mind just in case I needed it.

When I finished, he rose and poured a cup of coffee and offered it to me. I declined. He took a sip, then said, "There's been a gang of rustlers working along the border, Mr. Colter. Usually over Caldwell way." He nodded to the two deputies by the stove. "Me and the boys here been looking for them. I don't know if this is the same bunch, because this is the first time I've heard them pull off something like this."

One of the deputies spoke up: "Ain't that spur the one that John Tolbert started using, Max?"

Tolbert! For some reason, the name sounded familiar. "I've heard the name before, Sheriff. Who is this Tolbert hombre?"

The sheriff shrugged. "He's one of the buyers in

town. He works for a big meat company in Chicago. All the others use the spur here in Dodge, but Tolbert is young and full of vinegar. He'll use the spur closest to the herd, so as not to run any more fat off them beeves than he has to. Makes him look better to the company, you know.''

Then I remembered. Tolbert—he was the buyer missing the day before, when the other buyers and I were having our beers over in the Long Branch. He was out looking at a herd then. My herd. ''Where do you think I could find Mr. Tolbert, Sheriff?''

He studied me narrowly, instantly surmising my intentions. ''Why don't you just let me talk to him, Mr. Colter? To be honest, I ain't particularly interested in havin' no trouble in my town.'' He grinned. ''In fact, I wouldn't mind seeing one crew of you Texas wildcats leaving Dodge without either burning a saloon down or carrying off half our ladies.''

The two deputies slowly eased around to face us, but the move was unnecessary. Max Smith's easygoing nature and blunt humor told me he was a man to be trusted. Besides, we had enough trouble already. We didn't need any more. ''I'd take that to be right hospitable of you, Sheriff. I don't want to cause you gents any trouble at all. I just want my herd back. And,'' I added, a grin on my face, ''I'd like to leave Dodge with your ladies and your saloons in fine shape.''

The easy grin broadened on the sheriff's face. ''I'm right pleased to hear that, Mr. Colter. Where you fellers bedding down?''

''Since we're about busted, I reckon it'll be just

outside of town. We still got grub. Just look for the wagon.''

The constant saddle time for the last two days had worn the entire crew to a nub, and after a hasty supper of cold biscuits and hot coffee, every last one crawled into his bedroll, but not before Blackjack and Emmett Baldow bellyached about not having money to spend in the saloons in Dodge.

I sat and leaned back against a wagon wheel and tried to relax. I was restless and uncomfortable, as much from my impatience to hear from the sheriff as from finding myself in the unusual situation of having time on my hands.

Finally I dozed, and although I jerked awake several times as the fire died, I was slumbering restlessly when the thud of hoofbeats awakened me. The fire was only a bed of winking coals.

Jumping to my feet, I crouched in the shadows of the wagon, my .44 drawn and cocked. I'd had my fill of these Kansas outlaws, and the next one who figured on getting rich off me would find himself the owner of a hundred and eighty grains of lead and his own private hole in the ground.

I made out the blurred shadows of a single rider. He pulled up a distance from the wagon. ''Colter? It's me, Sheriff Smith.''

I grabbed a couple of cow chips from the possum belly and tossed them on the ashes. I kicked coals over the chips, which quickly broke into weak, guttering flames. ''Come on in, Sheriff.''

"I got my deputies out behind me. All right to call them in?"

That was the first signal that things were not altogether right. "Call them in."

He did, and the three of them rode in. The sheriff dismounted while his deputies remained in the saddle. The sheriff's face was grim.

Most of the crew had already stirred from their bedrolls and were sitting up and listening when I asked, "You find my cattle?"

"Well, now, Mr. Colter, that's a right interesting question. I found someone's cattle. Whether they be yours or not, I'm wondering."

"Sounds like you got something on your mind, Sheriff."

"I do, Mr. Colter. I got me some puzzling questions that I'd like to get some answers to."

His deputies sat motionless. I looked at him. "No more than I would like to get my herd back, Sheriff."

"A funny thing happened when I talked to Mr. Tolbert, Colter. He bought a herd. He showed me the bill of sale. Seven dollars a head for twelve hundred head of cattle, but the funny part was that the man he bought them from was Shadrach Colter, the gent you say you are."

My crew muttered in surprise, and I quickly saw just what had happened. But how it came about, I couldn't figure out yet. I shook my head and said, "I got ten men here who'll tell you who I am, Sheriff." I patted my shirt pocket. "I have a letter here from my boss on the Flying A that will identify me. And I didn't sell any cattle to any Mr. Tolbert.''

He eyed the crew, who had risen from their blankets and stood listening intently. ''No doubt about that, Mr. Colter, but I reckon whoever this other yahoo might be could very well have ten men swear *he* was Shadrach Colter.'' He nodded at the letter in my shirt pocket. ''Meaning no offense, but anyone can write a letter.''

My crew muttered in protest, but Sheriff Smith was right. We can say we are whoever we want to be, and anyone can write a letter. ''I figure there's only one way to solve this, Sheriff.''

He arched an eyebrow. ''What do you suggest?''

''Take me to see Mr. Tolbert.''

''That's what I planned on doing.''

I glanced at his deputies, and he grinned sheepishly. ''I always believe in being prepared, Mr. Colter.''

Cal stepped forward. ''Can I help, boss?''

''Saddle me a horse, Cal.''

''One for me too, son,'' Ed said, stepping from the shadows with his Winchester.

Cal glanced at me and I nodded. Ed had been part of the ranch longer than all the rest of us. He was entitled to go with me. Sawtooth stood nearby, as always a big grin on his face. ''Look after things,'' I told him.

He nodded. ''Don't worry, boss.''

The regulator clock hanging on the wall struck one o'clock when we entered the hotel. Sheriff Smith led the way up to the second floor, where a door opened even before we reached it. John Tolbert was waiting for us.

Inside the room he shook his head. "This isn't the gentleman I bought the herd from, Sheriff."

Ed bristled. "You sayin' he ain't Shad Colter?"

Tolbert shook his head emphatically. "Oh, no. All I'm saying is that I've never seen this gentleman before."

"This other man. What'd he look like?" I asked.

"Not much different from any of the other cowboys coming through here. About your size, sandy hair—"

Ed interrupted: "Freckles?"

Tolbert nodded. "Why, yes."

"That was him," Ed said, shaking his head vigorously. "That was the one who come out and claimed to be the sheriff."

"You ever see this sandy-haired jasper before, Mr. Tolbert?" Sheriff Smith asked.

"Never have, Sheriff. Sorry. But he did have a paper authorizing him to sell the herd, all notarized and everything."

"Just where is this paper, Mr. Tolbert?" I asked.

Tolbert looked at Sheriff Smith and shrugged. "In my desk." He pulled a metal box from a drawer and thumbed through the files. "Here it is." He handed it to me.

I studied the document. A signature purporting to be Carrie Alexander's gave Shadrach Colter the right to sell the herd in the name of the Flying A. I noticed that the document had been notarized in Caldwell, Kansas, by an attorney named J. Silas Witherspoon.

"Didn't that seem strange?" I asked, handing the document to Sheriff Smith. "If the Flying A is in Texas, why was this notarized in Caldwell?"

Sheriff Smith narrowed his eyes as he handed the document to John Tolbert.

"Simple," Tolbert replied. "The owner caught the train for Wichita and St. Louis in Caldwell. She sent someone here with the herd." He shook his head and turned to the sheriff. "I'm sorry about all this, Sheriff, but I didn't do anything wrong, and my company appears to be the legal owner of the herd, which is halfway to Chicago by now."

"That's good enough for me," the sheriff said.

"Hold on a minute here, Sheriff." I disliked the finality in his voice. "What about my herd?"

He smiled easily, an affable, soothing grin that he must have been practicing for many years. "Let's leave Mr. Tolbert be and go over to my office and iron out the details."

Ed looked at me. I nodded.

Tolbert spoke up. His tone was apologetic. "I'm sorry, cowboy, but you can see my position. That other gentleman provided all the legal papers necessary to close the deal. I hope you catch the man. But maybe some good can come to you from this raw deal."

"Such as?"

"My company has been trying to get the Atchison Topeka and Santa Fe to run a line down into the Texas Panhandle, maybe on through to Houston. When they see what kind of trouble such a spur could head off, they just might be prompted to go ahead with it.''

I couldn't resist a wry grin. ''Doesn't do me much good right now.'' I followed the sheriff from the room. If I couldn't take the legal way, I'd figure out some other, but one way or another, I wasn't returning without the herd money.

The sheriff was hog-tied and ready for the iron. ''Unless you can get me some kind of definite proof,'' he said, ''I can't do nothing legally.'' He hesitated. ''I believe you are who you say you are. But you can see yourself that I can do nothing until you get me some hard proof that you're Shadrach Colter. I won't stop working on this, although it'll have to be in my spare time. If I run across anything, I'll get in touch.''

Ed fussed all the way back to the camp. I ignored him, for my thoughts were filled with my next move. I couldn't afford to waste time. The rustlers were out spending the herd money right now, and the longer I waited, the less I could recover for the Flying A.

Back in camp I squatted with a cup of coffee and considered what to do next. The document was notarized in Caldwell, so my first step was to visit the lawyer and see what he knew about the man claiming to be me.

''What now, Shad?'' Ed hunkered down beside me, his elbows resting on his knees.

''Reckon we'll push out at sunrise for Texas. You boys head on down.''

''What about you?''

''I'm going to Caldwell. Our rustlers came from over

there, or at least they passed through there. I'll see what I can find, and then I'll catch up with you."

He grunted. "We're running low on grub."

"Sign for the Flying A. Most places will give us credit."

"I don't mean to buck you, Shad, but you might need us in Caldwell. No telling what you might run into."

There was no real reason for them to head back to Texas at sunup, and a few days more or less would hurt nothing. "Okay by me. If we come up at a dead end over there, we'll head back."

Ed nodded and crawled under the wagon into his bedroll.

I glanced at the stars. About three, I guessed. I crawled into my bedroll, but sleep evaded me. Our drive to Dodge was no secret back in Sweetwater Creek, so any number of no-goods could have cooked up this plan, but one thing puzzled me, one thing no one could have known. My name. Shadrach. All they knew me by in Sweetwater Creek was Shad.

Try as I might, I couldn't shake the feeling that there was more to this than just rustling. *Maybe*, I told myself as I pulled my hat down over my eyes, *maybe I'll find some answers in Caldwell.*

Chapter Ten

Take away the name of the town, and Caldwell, Kansas, could just as well be Wichita, Abilene, or Dodge. On each side of the dusty main street, board and batten buildings, mud-chinked cabins, and weather-worn tents offered dry goods, medicines, canned goods, whiskey, and various services ranging from hot baths to tending mules to gambling.

We pulled up in front of the saloon, where I asked a cowboy heading inside, "You know a lawyer named Witherspoon?"

He pointed to an unpainted two-story building across the street. "Yep. He's got his office over the butcher store there."

I pulled up in front of the butcher store and hitched my horse. I didn't see any stairs on the side of the building. "You boys wait out here for me," I told them.

The odor of stale fat and lard smacked me in the face when I opened the door. Along one side of the room stretched a meat rack from which hung several halves of beef. At the far end of the room was the counter, upon one end of which stood a stuffed elk with antlers six feet from point to point. At the other end of the counter, a butcher swung a meat cleaver as he broke the halves into quarters.

A sign hanging on the wall next to a stairway indicated that Witherspoon's office was upstairs. I pushed through the glass-paneled door at the head of the stairs.

A middle-aged man tending to overweight looked up from behind the desk as I entered. He nodded to the two chairs along the wall. "Be with you in a minute, mister. Have a seat."

I watched as he made a show of signing several documents with exaggerated flourishes. Finally, he pushed them aside in a neat stack and turned to me. "What can I do for you, sir?"

"You can notarize documents, isn't that true?"

"Most assuredly, sir, most assuredly." He extended his hand and smiled broadly. "Just what kind of document did you wish to have notarized?"

"I don't have one. I want to ask you about one that you notarized a couple of weeks back."

His frown faded. "That's impossible."

"I lost twelve hundred head of cattle because of the document you notarized, so I've got some questions I want answers for." Quickly, I related all that had happened. And I finished, "I reckon you can see why I need to know all about this jasper who called himself Shadrach Colter."

He shook his head emphatically and drew himself

into a big puff of hot air. "As I said, quite impossible. Those records are private and sacrosanct by law."

Sighing in frustration at his crawfishing, I pulled my gun. "Well, it might be sacrosanct by law, but by my .44 it will be possible." I cocked the hammer. His face blanched, and he plopped down in his chair and scrabbled through his desk for his records.

"Here it is," he blubbered, shoving the record book across the desk to me.

I looked at the document. It was simply a copy of the one that John Tolbert had shown me. I cut my eyes back at the lawyer. "What did he look like?"

He opened his mouth.

I waved the muzzle of my revolver. "The truth, Mr. Witherspoon."

J. Silas Witherspoon swallowed hard and wiped at the perspiration beading on his forehead. "Young, blond hair, about your size."

"Freckles?"

He nodded vigorously. "Yes."

"And what about this signature? The woman who signed Carrie Alexander's name, what did she look like?"

"She was a blonde too. Small." He held the edge of his hand against his chest. "She came to about here on me. Never saw her before. Him I have, around town here two or three times, but I never saw *her*."

Holstering my revolver, I thanked him and left.

The crew having gathered around me at the hitching rail, I told them of what I had learned. "So, it looks like we got us some more looking around to do,'' I finished. ''We'll meet back here.''

After repeating the description of the two, I scattered the crew around town, counting on the outside chance that one or both were still knocking around Caldwell.

For once, luck decided to ride with us.

Sawtooth came rushing back about thirty minutes later. He had seen a young man fitting the description in the Someday Saloon, bucking the tiger at the faro table.

''Let's go, Ed,'' I said, cutting across the street. ''You other boys wait here.''

''Aren't you gonna git the sheriff?''

I shook my head. ''What could he do? No more than the sheriff over at Dodge. No, I'll handle this myself.''

Pausing just inside the batwing doors so that my eyes could adjust to the light, I studied the young man still at the faro table. Sandy hair and freckles, and he was throwing money around faster than he could shovel out a stable. ''What about it, Ed? That him?''

''That's him, by jeebers. That's him.''

''Okay. You wait here.''

I made my way across the room to stand across the felt-covered table from the man. He glanced at me and returned to the game, dropping a handful of chips on the ace of spades. The dealer pulled up a five of hearts to reveal a four of clubs.

The young man snorted. ''Blast!''

The dealer grinned. ''Maybe next time, cowboy.''

He shook his head. ''Ole Lady Luck, she just ain't smiling on me today.''

"Could be you've run out your string," I said softly.

Surprised by my butting in, he glared at me. "What's that you say, mister?"

"I said that maybe you've used up all your luck by running off someone else's cattle."

His hand froze in midair over the king of spades. His eyes narrowed. "Who are you?"

"I'm Shad Colter, the *real* Shad Colter, and you're going with me to have a talk with the sheriff."

He lowered his hand slowly and stepped back from the table. "Not in this lifetime."

"Don't be foolish. You got your whole life ahead of you. Just unfasten your gun belt and drop it to the floor."

His eyes held mine, level and steady. I knew with a sickening dread that he was going to play out his hand, and that his luck was going to be just as bad with his gun as with his cards.

The saloon had grown silent, its patrons pulling aside and watching with expectation. The only sound was the click-click-click of the roulette wheel winding down.

"Cowboy, you either drop the gun or use it. One way or another, I'm taking you to the sheriff."

A crooked grin curled one side of his lips. "You brag too much. Make your play."

His hand flashed to his revolver, but I was faster. I caught him square in the chest just as he cleared leather. The impact of the slugs spun him around and slammed him to the floor. He was dead by the time I knelt at his side.

I looked up at the crowd pressing in around us. "Anyone know him?"

"He called hisself Buster," a bar patron said.

"That it?"

"All I ever heard."

At that moment the sheriff came rushing in, his gun drawn. I explained what had happened and the bartender verified my story. I then told the sheriff about the stolen herd and my business with the sheriff in Dodge.

The sheriff searched the dead man for identification. All he could find was a wallet with a wad of money. Then he told me, "Don't leave town till I check with the sheriff over in Dodge."

"I don't plan on it, Sheriff." I nodded at the wallet. Ed had come to stand by my side. "This jasper has over eight thousand dollars that belongs to my boss back in Texas, and I don't plan on moving south one step until I have it strapped around my waist."

The sheriff's eyes grew wide when I said eight thousand dollars. He opened the wallet and quickly leafed through the bills. "Well, he don't have the eight thousand here." He tossed me the wallet. "See for yourself, then give it back. If that there belongs to you, you'll get it soon enough."

There was only five hundred and seventy-six dollars in the wallet. I looked at Ed and then at the faro dealer, who watched impassively from behind his table. I tossed the wallet back to the sheriff and said to the faro dealer, "How much did this jasper lose?"

He shrugged. "Not much. A couple hundred."

"This kid come in here much?"

The faro dealer stared at me with bored eyes. "Seen him a couple of times."

"You know him by name?"

"Nope." He puckered his lips as if he was considering something. He nodded to the hotel lobby that adjoined the saloon. "Saw the kid come downstairs a while ago. Could be he has a room over there."

When I turned around, two men were carrying the kid from the saloon. The sheriff followed.

Ed and I talked to the hotel clerk. The kid had signed the register with just one name—Buster. Accompanied by the clerk, I searched Buster's room, but there was nothing, not even any personal items.

Outside on the boardwalk in front of the hotel, I paused and looked up and down the street. "Well, Ed, what do you think?"

He grunted and shifted his weight to his good leg. "Looks like we're boxed in. What about the woman? Maybe we can find her."

"She probably took the first stage back to Abilene or Wichita and lost herself in some two-bit saloon."

"So we're at a dead end?"

That was the way it looked to me, but there had to be something else, something we were overlooking, something I had forgotten. Where was the remainder of the eight thousand? Had the kid hidden it? Or did he have a partner?

The sun was sinking low. The boys over at the hitching rail were growing restless. I guessed maybe it was time to hang up my hat and take my licking. Then a horse at the hitching rail nickered. That was it—his horse. That's what I had forgotten. He would have stabled his horse before checking into the hotel. I looked around Caldwell. The open doors of the town's only livery yawned at me from the end of the street.

The hostler remembered the kid well because when he rode in, his horse was heavily lathered and sucking air from being ridden so hard. The young man had leaped off the horse and tossed the hostler the reins. And after a curt "Take care of him, old man," he'd headed up the street to the saloon.

"Here's all he had," the old man said, pointing to Buster's saddle and bridle after pocketing the coin I had given him to loosen his tongue.

"No saddlebags?"

"No, sirree. Jist the clothes on his back."

"Did he come back here at all?"

"Nope. But I did see him talking to a stranger just before he hit the saloon."

My hopes leaped. "This stranger, what did he look like? Can you describe him?"

"Reckon not. Too far away." He gestured to his eyes. "The old peepers are getting weak in my old age," he crackled. "But not too weak to see that he was riding one of them Appaloosa horses."

An Appaloosa! And as far as I was concerned, only one man rode an Appaloosa—Jim Farley!

"This stranger. You happen to notice if he was wearing a black vest?"

The ancient hostler studied on the question for a moment. Slowly he nodded. "Best I can recollect, he did. But I ain't certain sure."

Chapter Eleven

Ed frowned at me. The arch of his eyebrow told me that we were thinking the same thing. "You don't figure . . . ?"

Certainly I was aware that many cowpokes rode Appaloosas, but somehow I knew beyond doubt that the Appaloosa the old hostler had spotted belonged to Jim Farley. Suddenly, a large chunk of the puzzle slid into place. Jim Farley had sworn to get even with me, and so he dreamed up this rustling scheme. I nodded. "Yep. Sure as night follows day."

"That button sure holds hate for a long time," Ed said as we headed back to the butcher store and our waiting crew. "What do you figure on doing now?"

"Find Farley. We'll spread out the crew and tear Caldwell apart."

I sent the men through the town, but no one turned up any trace of Jim Farley. "Not a sign of him," Ed reported. "Nobody I talked to even saw the Appaloosa." The rest of the crew echoed his assertion.

Well, I've got to admit that Jim Farley had me puzzled. Only a ghost could have drifted in and out of town as he had without being spotted. But he wasn't a ghost. He was flesh and blood, and someone had to have spotted him. A chilling thought struck me. Could one of the crew be working with Farley? That could explain why no one had seen him. My first thoughts went to Blackjack and Emmett Baldow, but I quickly dismissed them. The two were contrary, but they did everything I asked. I couldn't believe they were involved with Farley.

Back at the camp, Ed squatted by the fire and eyed me as I hunkered down with a cup of coffee. He spoke up: ''I reckon we ought to head on back to Sweetwater Creek. It looks like he's done give us the slip.''

I sipped the thick, steaming coffee and leaned back against the wagon wheel. I tried to relax, but all I could think of was the missing money. ''Reckon you're right, Ed. You take 'em back. I'm going to hang around a mite longer. I'll catch up with you.''

My words surprised him. He rose and shifted his weight to his good leg as he massaged the gimpy one. ''That don't make sense, Shad. Why, the man's done disappeared with no trace. What makes you think you can find him when none of us could whip up the least sign of him?''

''One man can sometimes find out a lot more than a whole passel of yapping faces.''

''Well, not here,'' he replied testily. ''You're just wasting time if you think you can find him.''

I frowned at the sudden agitation in his voice. ''What the deuce is bothering you, Ed?''

''Nothing. It's just—well, I don't feel good about

taking these boys back by myself. I'm just a cook. We still got enough valuables for someone to jump us."

"You don't think I should follow Farley? Try to save what money I can for the ranch?"

He stared at me for several seconds, then he ducked his head. "Shucks, Shad, sure I do. I was just being selfish, I reckon." He nodded to the south. "I just don't cotton to the idea of being out there without a gun like yours behind us." He gave me a sheepish grin.

"Don't worry, Ed. I'll catch you before you reach the Cimarron. Besides, you got Sawtooth and Cal Stone. They're good boys."

He shook his head. "Well, I can't say I'm any too sold on the idea, but if that's what you want us to do, then by golly, I reckon we'll certain do it."

The crew pulled out before sunrise. I watched until they disappeared over the first rise, and then I turned the buckskin back to Caldwell. During the night I had given much thought to Jim Farley and his clever plan for rustling the herd.

But a nagging thought continued to worry me. Sure, the plan was slick, and that was the problem. It was too slick for Jim Farley to have initiated it. Here was a wet-behind-the-ears kid who was dumb enough to rustle from his own brand while riding the only Appaloosa in the county—or possibly in the state, for that matter. Anyone who pulled such a foolish stunt had to be a couple of pickles shy of a barrelful.

I pulled up at the hitching rail in front of the Someday Saloon, a likely spot for a man like Jim Farley to frequent. The town had three more saloons. I planned on visiting each of them, and then I would decide on my next step.

One thing I believed beyond question was that Jim Farley had not planned the rustling scheme. He was working for someone, and I was bound and determined to find out that someone's identity, even if I had to roast the boy's brains over a fire.

Visits to the first three saloons proved fruitless, but at the fourth, a pear-shaped bartender remembered a man in a black leather vest.

"Yep," he said, wiping at the bar with a jovial smile plastered on his face, "I seen him a few days back."

"He say where he was heading?"

He eyed me suspiciously. "I don't ask questions, mister. I just sell whiskey and beer."

I shook my head in disgust. "Thanks, anyway."

"This guy," the bartender said. "What'd he do? Shoot someone?"

I laughed. "Nope. Nothing so exciting. He's just a friend I met up Montana way. He told me he hung around here sometimes."

A wry grin curled the bartender's fat lips. "He musta got a bunch of friends. You're the second one in two days asking about him."

I suppressed a surge of excitement. "Is that so?"

"Yep."

"What'd you tell him? About my friend, I mean?"

He relaxed and grinned at me. "Same thing I'm telling you. This jasper in the black vest said he was heading up to Wichita. The only reason I remember is he plunked down a twenty-dollar gold piece for a couple of bottles of Old Commissary whiskey to tote along with him. Didn't even wait for no change.''

"I'm much obliged," I said, wondering about the man who had asked about Farley. "By the way, this other cowpoke who asked about my friend, what'd he look like? I might know him, or I might run into him on the trail. We could ride together. I'm not anxious to be by my lonesome with all these raiders you Kansas folks got riding across the prairies.''

The bartender laughed at my observation of Kansas outlaws. "You're right about that, stranger." He paused in wiping the bar, his brow wrinkled in thought. "A young kid—no, it was an old man. He limped when he walked.''

"You sure?''

"Think so, but I ain't certain. You park your carcass behind here and try to remember all them faces. They run together after a spell, but I'm almost certain that's who done the asking.''

"Thanks," I said. "You been a big help.''

Outside, I considered what I had learned and tried to understand what it meant. Had Ed Boswell questioned the bartender? Or was the bartender mistaken? If he was telling the truth, why did Ed lie and say he had heard nothing?

Perhaps the old man had simply forgotten.

That's how old age happened to old Ned. He just woke up one morning and couldn't remember a thing that had taken place within the last five years. He could remember when he was a button, but not how the sunset had looked the day before.

Was that what was happening to Ed? And could that be the reason he hadn't wanted to shepherd the crew back to Texas?

Those questions would have to wait. Right now, I had to head for Wichita and Jim Farley. But first I stopped by the sheriff's office and picked up the Flying A money.

I reached Wichita early the next morning. Pulling into the first livery, I paid the hostler four bits for feed and a stall for my buckskin. I looked around the livery but saw no Appaloosa.

Slowly I made my way up one side of the street and down the other, stopping in at each saloon and questioning each bartender. No luck.

Disappointed, I ordered a beer in the last saloon and sipped at it while I gazed around the smoke-filled room, at the same time trying to decide on my next move. Suddenly, my eyes locked on a face at a card table at the rear of the room. It belonged to Bill Hollier, Jim Farley's partner back on the Flying A.

I squinted into the smoke to be sure my eyes weren't playing tricks on me. The man *was* Bill Hollier. I started toward him.

At that moment two ragtag cowpokes jumped back from a nearby table and started blazing away at each other. Bill looked up, and his eyes met mine. A stray slug shattered a beer mug on the table by my side. Another hummed past me. Shots came from behind.

It looked like someone else wanted to get into the fight, and I hit the floor, overturning a table on the way down.

The flimsy table wouldn't stop a hundred-and-eighty-grain slug, but it would hide me more or less. If those crazy yahoos shooting at each other couldn't see me, maybe they wouldn't fire in my direction.

I peered from around the bottom of the table, trying to spot Bill amid the tangle of overturned tables and chairs. All I could see was a welter of bodies huddled under tables and clustered against the walls, climbing over each other in an effort to reach the door just like a litter of piglets fighting to nurse.

Just as suddenly as the shooting began, it ceased. I remained as I was, perfectly willing to let someone else stand up first. A murmur of voices began, and the intensity swelled until someone yelled, "Get the sheriff!"

Footsteps sounded behind me, and I looked around. Several men were rushing across the room to the fallen cowboys. I rose slowly, my eyes scanning the room for Bill, but he had disappeared. All I saw was an open door at the rear of the saloon.

The door opened into an alley, but the worn-down path indicated that the rear door served as many customers as the front one. There was no way to pick up a single man's sign amidst the clutter of boot tracks on the packed ground.

I headed for the livery. Bill had spotted me; of that, I was certain, and if he were mixed up in this scheme, his first thought would be to shed himself of this town.

Sure enough, at the third livery, I learned that a man fitting Bill's description had taken the north road out of Wichita less than fifteen minutes earlier.

From the top of my buckskin I studied the road. "Where does it go?"

The hostler looked at the road. "Abilene."

As I looked down at him, a grin came to my face. I remembered C.H. telling me that Jim and Bill were out of Abilene. He had said it just in passing, and it had completely slipped my mind till now. "You say Abilene?"

"Yep. About a two-day ride. You need any grub, Sam Wainwright across the street has got the best prices in town."

Instead of digging my heels into my buckskin, I deliberately took my time. Bill would not get away from me. I knew where he was bound.

At Wainwright's store I bought some crackers and three cans of tomatoes. I eyed a bag of coffee wistfully, but I knew there would be no time for a fire and the luxury of boiling coffee.

That night I spotted a camp on the bank of a small creek. Leaving the buckskin behind, I slipped close to make sure it was Bill's, then returned to my own cold camp, wolfed down some crackers and a can of tomatoes, and climbed back into the saddle.

Let Bill think he had given me the slip. I would be waiting for him in Abilene. And I planned to follow him right into Jim Farley's lap.

*   *   *

Bill rode in late the next afternoon, a couple of hours earlier than I had expected. He had pushed his horse, and the lathered animal showed it. Bill pulled up to the Stockman Hotel and went inside. I peered through the window and watched as the young man spoke with the room clerk, nodded, and went into the adjoining saloon.

I moved over to the next window, which was several feet from the first, and looked in. Bill wove his way through the tables and climbed a flight of stairs. He turned left at the top and disappeared into the first room.

Flipping the rawhide loop off the hammer of my .44, I hurried inside and, ignoring the patrons at the bar, started up the stairs.

A door upstairs opened, and suddenly Jim Farley and Bill Hollier appeared at the top of the stairs. They stiffened when they saw me. In the next instant they grabbed for their guns. I leveled mine first. "Hold on, boys. You remember what happened last time."

Their hands froze.

The icy click of a cocking hammer behind me broke the silence. "I'd say that you should just hold on too, mister."

I kept my gun trained on the two rustlers. "Whatever you say, cowboy. But if you don't mind, why don't you just get me the sheriff."

A couple of snickers sounded from across the silent room.

"Well, you got lucky, mister, 'cause that's exactly who I am."

I gave the voice a quick glance. A grim-faced man had a .44 trained on me. He wore a badge on his chest.

"Now suppose you just stick that hogleg of yours back where it belongs," he said, his voice low but firm.

"Sheriff, you won't have any trouble with me, but first listen to what I have to say." I gestured with the muzzle of my gun at the two nervous men at the top of the stairs. Bill Hollier was shaking noticeably. "Those two rustled some cattle from me over near Dodge." Quickly, I explained all that had happened.

"You got proof of what you say, I guess?"

I nodded to Jim. "You'll find a large sum of money on him, or in his room. I don't know how much is left, but he got over eight thousand dollars for the beeves."

Bill spoke up: "What? How much?" He glared at Jim, who whispered, "I'll explain, pal. Later."

But something had agitated Bill. Then I understood.

Bill continued: "Eight thousand. Colter said eight thousand. You told me we got only four thousand."

Jim threw us a nervous glance. "Shut up, dummy!" he snarled at his partner.

Bill glared at Jim. "You always cheated me, but I was too dumb to realize it." He glanced at me and the sheriff. "Well, it's over with now. I don't know if I can get out of this or not, but if I do, if I ever see you again, I'll blow your head clean off." He looked back to the sheriff. "Colter's right, Sheriff. We rustled his herd."

* * *

I rode out of Abilene early the next morning with a money belt snugged around my waist. Jim and Bill sat in a cell awaiting trial and, in all probability, a rope, which was a fate long overdue the two men. I had the herd money—at least, all that was left, only two thousand dollars, nowhere near the five thousand due the bank. And only about fifteen hundred of the money was the Flying A's. The remainder was the Box K's and Circle Eight's.

So, any way I could figure, the ranch needed another thirty-five hundred dollars to buy up the mortgage. Might as well be a hundred thousand.

I caught up with the wagon and crew at the Canadian River. They had camped in the middle of a grove of cottonwoods, and they spotted me as I dropped down off the prairie into the river valley. Several rode up to meet me.

Ed handed me a cup of steaming coffee as I squatted by the fire. ''Well?''

That single word summed up the expressions on all their faces. I nodded. ''I got what was left of the money.''

The grins on their faces faded. Blackjack stepped forward. He studied me narrowly. ''What do you mean, what was left?'' Emmett Baldow pulled up beside Blackjack.

I glanced at Ed, remembering what the bartender back in Caldwell had told me about talking to an old man. There would be time later to ask him, time when we would be alone.

"Might as well give it to you boys straight. Jim Farley was behind it. We ended up with only two thousand dollars." I patted the money belt around my waist. "Right here."

Cal Stone muttered in disbelief. "How does anyone spend that much in just a few days?"

"I could," Sawtooth said in a weak effort to lighten the depression that had settled over the crew. But no one laughed, and the mood deepened.

I told them what I had learned: "Farley paid the kid in Caldwell a thousand dollars to act like the sheriff. The kid must have paid the woman and riders from his share. From talking to the saloons around Abilene, I found out that Farley lost over five thousand in a couple days."

"Well, at least there's enough there to get our pay," Blackjack observed.

"Yeah. And I'm ready to take it and hightail for the nearest saloon," Emmett said.

The crew looked at me hopefully.

"Yep. There's money enough for your pay." I paused and studied them. Throughout the ride from Abilene, I had dreaded this moment.

"What about it, boss? You gonna pay us now?" Cal asked.

I took a deep breath and stood up. "Boys, the ranch owes you money, and I guarantee you'll get every last penny, but I want to take this money back to Miss Alexander so she can pay some on her note and try to keep the ranch afloat. I plan on letting her use the wages I got coming, and I'm asking you to do the same.''

One of the crew said, ''I was planning on a new saddle and boots. These I got on got nothing but paper for soles.''

''We all got good plans for the wages. I know that. And I'm not asking you to do anything I wouldn't do.''

Blackjack spoke up: ''She don't need the money. All them rich ranchers got plenty to spare.'' He looked around at the crew. ''I say, pay us first, then use what's left.''

There were a few mutters of agreement until Cal Stone said, ''If you wanta let Miss Carrie use our pay, boss, it's okay by me.''

''Me too,'' Sawtooth chimed in.

''Well, not me,'' Blackjack barked.

''Me neither,'' Emmett Baldow said.

I studied the two men. ''The money isn't mine to pay you with. I'm taking it to Miss Alexander. If she wants to pay you, then that's her business.''

A few of the men nodded, and I considered the matter closed.

Later, a knot of men approached. Blackjack and Emmett Baldow were in the lead. Three men followed behind. They stopped in front of me.

''We wanta talk, Colter.''

I saw trouble coming head-on and my muscles tensed, but I tried to appear relaxed. ''I'm listening.''

Cal Stone and Sawtooth walked up, curious as to the topic of a conversation that drew almost every man in camp. Suddenly Emmett Baldow drew down on the two men. "Hold it right there," he said. "This don't concern you two. It's between us and Colter."

Blackjack kept his eyes on me. The three men behind him stepped up beside the slender man. Off to the left, the remaining two crew members watched idly from their bedrolls.

I rose slowly. Just as slowly, I eased the rawhide loop off the hammer of my .44. "Suppose you just tell me what's stuck in your craw."

"We decided that we're entitled to the whole two thousand," Blackjack said, a sneer in his voice.

Ed came to stand beside me.

I replied in a soft voice, "Four to two is good odds, men, but I'm warning you—I'll put you four down before any of you can clear leather."

A couple of the cowpokes glanced around nervously.

"How about six to two, Colter," a voice said as the other two crew members stepped up beside the four.

I grinned. "I reckon that'll make it a lot more interesting. How about it, Ed?" I said, never taking my eyes off the six men facing me. "You take the two on the right. I'll take care of the other four."

"Durn tootin'. And right pleased to do it. No one is gonna take from this brand."

Blackjack's sneer broadened. He started to say more, but I yelled "Now!" and grabbed for my gun. I blew holes in the first two men's thighs, and drilled the right shoulder of the next two. Within four seconds, four men sprawled on the ground. The other two grabbed at the sky like they was trying to climb into the clouds.

I turned my gun on Emmett Baldow. "Your turn, Baldow."

He gulped, and quickly shoved his gun back into his holster. I glared at him and the remaining two crew members. "Hardware in the wagon!" Without hesitation, each shucked his gun belt and tossed it in the chuckwagon.

"Now, Baldow, patch up those four, and be fast about it."

The next morning I sent Ed and the wagon across the river with Cal and Sawtooth accompanying it.

"You can't leave us without protection," Emmett Baldow whined when he saw my intention. "There's Injuns about." The others looked up at me, their faces sullen.

I stared at him with cold eyes. "You'd best be glad I left you alive. When you come back to the Flying A to pick up your wages, don't hang around. You've got no welcome at the table." I glared at the others. "That goes for every last one of you."

Without another word, I wheeled the buckskin around and headed across the Canadian. I had never objected to anyone trying to kick over the traces. Sometimes it was the thing to do because of the good changes that could come about. But common thievery was something else.

During the remainder of the ride back to the ranch, I had time to think—about myself, about the ranch, about Carrie Alexander. And the more I thought, the angrier I became. We reached the ranch just before sundown.

Shadows gathered in the east and slowly rolled across the sky toward us. Ed went straight to his cookshack, and I sent the two boys to unhitch the team and turn them out to graze. I headed for the ranch house, the two thousand dollars still strapped around my waist.

I saw Carrie peeking around the edge of the curtain in the front window. She dropped it hastily when she saw me looking at her.

Her angry words the day before we had pulled out still rang in my ears. My only regret was that I had not returned with enough money to pay off the mortgage, a debt I had obligated myself to settle for old C.H. I would have liked nothing better than to walk into her parlor, plop down eight thousand dollars, and then leave.

With some dismay, I knew I would stay until the end. That was the least I could do for C.H. It wouldn't be enough, but it was all I could do. Also, I had some advice for Carrie Alexander, words she wouldn't like, but ones she was sure going to hear.

She answered the door at my first knock. Without looking at her, I strode into the parlor, which was lit by light from a lantern that appeared to be freshly polished. I turned to face her, and the angry words I had rehearsed all day stuck in my throat.

I almost failed to recognize her. Instead of being in a prim and proper dress with all the San Francisco frills, a western woman in denims, cotton shirt, and boots faced me. And she was still right pretty.

Her cheeks colored when I continued to stare at her.

For one of the few times in my life, I was too flustered to speak.

"Well," she said softly, shrugging, "I knew I would look different, but I didn't think I would look so ugly that you couldn't say anything."

Without waiting for an answer, she left the room and returned with a pot of coffee and a platter full of twisted doughnuts. "Please sit down."

Remembering how particular she was about clean clothes, I said, "I'm fresh off the trail. I got two months worth of dirt sticking to me."

Pouring a cup of black coffee, she shook her head. "Don't worry about the furniture. That's what it's for, to be used and not just seen."

Her words surprised me, but I did as she said. She poured herself a cup and sat in a wing chair across the coffee table from me. "Here, try some doughnuts. Frank and Peewee even ate some of these, which is an accomplishment for me. Of course," she said, a blush of color in her cheeks, "they gave my first ones to the birds. Claimed the birds couldn't even fly after eating them."

To my amazement, the coffee was good, and the doughnuts were right tasty also. I looked at her, unable to believe what I was seeing. "I—" I was at a loss for words. She was not the same cold woman I had left behind two months earlier. What could have happened to bring about such a change?

She noticed my silence. Suddenly, we both felt awkward. Carrie lowered her head and said, "I finally understood what you tried to tell me that first day you came in here. I'm ashamed of the way I spoke to you before you left. I was petty, selfish.'' She glanced up at me and a mischievous smile played over her lips. ''I was just a brat.''

Well, she was the one who said it. I nodded and grinned back at her. ''Yes, ma'am, you were, but—'' I held a doughnut up and nodded to her attire. ''But I reckon you've made a heap of changes, and they all look to be for the better.''

She blushed. ''Thanks, Shad. I know you're wondering what happened.''

''I reckon I am.''

''The first couple of days after the herd pulled out, I had time to think. I was lonesome, so lonesome. Oh, Peewee and Frank were here, but when they weren't working, they stayed in the bunkhouse. When I invited them up for tea, they remained as long as I wanted them to, but I could tell they were uncomfortable the whole time.

''Then one night I remembered your saying I should pull my own weight.'' She paused, drew a deep breath, and looked me square in the eyes. ''Well, I might be a lot of things, but I'm not dumb. I decided to give your advice a chance.'' She held her arms out to the side. ''And here I am. And I've never been happier.''

I held out the cup to her. ''You make right good coffee too. And your doughnuts aren't no slouches, either.''

Her mood sobered. ''Do you forgive me for all those hateful things I said? I hope you do. I sincerely want you to.''

By now, I had completely forgotten my carefully rehearsed speech. In fact, I had forgotten that I had even rehearsed a speech. "It's all in the past, Carrie."

"Thank you, Shad," she said. "So is San Francisco. Now that you're back, I don't want to think about anything except the ranch and how we can build it back into something my father would be proud of."

Suddenly, the coffee lost its flavor, and I set the cup on the table. Now it was my turn to look her in the eye. "There's bad news about the herd, Carrie. You'd better grab hold of something, because it'll smack you between the eyes harder than if a mule kicked you."

Her face paled. For a moment, indecision flickered in her eyes, but finally a glint of determination settled in. She set her jaw. "What happened?"

I told her, leaving out nothing, sparing her nothing.

When I finished, she stared at me, struggling to contain the tears, but the lantern light glittered on those welling in her eyes. "So we have only about fifteen hundred dollars," she murmured.

"That's right."

"And the men have not been paid, you say."

"Right again."

She drew up her shoulders. "They must be paid first."

I laid my hand on hers. "Ed and me and Cal and Sawtooth decided to lend you our wages at no interest. That'll help some."

She tightened her fingers around mine. "But the others, the ones you left at the Canadian? They have money coming.'' She struggled to contain the tears filling her eyes.

''That they do, but I'd wager a twenty-dollar gold piece they won't mind waiting, either.''

Using the heel of her hands, she wiped the tears roughly from her eyes and looked at me. ''What should we do?''

''Tomorrow we go to Sweetwater Creek and see the bank. Fifteen hundred dollars should get you an extension on your note.''

She gave me a wan smile. ''And if it doesn't?''

I grinned and reached for another doughnut. ''We'll figure out something else.''

Slowly she nodded and reached for a doughnut too. ''Did you know that these doughnuts turn themselves over in the pot?'' she asked woodenly, tracing a fingernail along the corkscrew shape of the doughnut. ''I guess it's because of the way they're twisted around before you join them in a circle.''

She hurt inside. I could tell. But she was doing her best to face hard facts with grit and determination, the two qualities that make up the backbone of a Western man or woman. I've heard folks wonder at the stoicism of Westerners, at the detached, almost unemotional manner in which they view the atrocities common throughout our land. What these same folks fail to understand is that such emotions must be contained, for misery and sorrow dull the edge of vigilance. And a person must be vigilant if he or she wants to survive in the West.

I started to dunk my doughnut, but hesitated. Carrie

laughed, but it was forced. "Go ahead. Peewee showed me how to dunk. I like them that way." She dunked her doughnut in her coffee. "The first time I made doughnuts," she said, beginning to chatter to keep from crying, "they came out like rocks. I followed the recipe: lard, egg, baking soda, flour, and sugar. I left out the sour cream. Maybe that was it. Do you think so?"

"Could be," I said, sipping the coffee. "Could be." I knew nothing about cooking doughnuts, but I was perfectly content to sit there and listen to her talk all night if that was what it took to get her over the hump. If she made it until morning and still wanted to hang on to the ranch, then somewhere along the way, she had become a Western woman.

She made it.

Next morning bright and early, we rode into town, me on my buckskin and Carrie on a docile little paint gelding about fourteen hands high. Although she was not ready to give riding exhibitions in a circus, she rode adequately. Her face lit up when I nodded my approval. And I felt like busting the buttons off my shirt.

"I've even learned to saddle him myself," she said, her voice bubbly and lively. "I've ridden every day, but sometimes I get sore if I ride too much."

I laughed. "We all do."

Neither of us let on that we were concerned about the bank's response to our request. While extensions were routinely granted, both of us feared that Williford

Perkins would somehow use the lack of funds against Carrie.

We rode into town and went straight to the bank. With a mixture of relief and concern, we discovered that Perkins was at a meeting of the town council.

The bank clerk, Walter Markby, was a man in his early thirties. He nodded and said, "I can help you, Miss Alexander. I've worked here in the bank over ten years, even before Mr. Perkins took it over."

Carrie handed him the money and explained her predicament.

He took the money and grinned broadly. "Certainly we can extend your mortgage with this payment. We have made such a practice for years."

The bank teller wrote up a document granting Carrie an additional two months. With a big smile of her own, she folded the document into her pocket.

"We're going to celebrate when we get home," she said as she climbed into the saddle. Her dazzling smile made my head spin.

But Williford Perkins broke up our little celebration when he showed up at the Flying A just before sundown.

Chapter Twelve

The entire crew had gathered around the piano in the parlor, enjoying Carrie's music. Once or twice, Sawtooth or some other brave soul would attempt to accompany her with the words of a church hymn or some popular little ditty.

Carrie glanced up at me and smiled. A warm flush burned my ears. For a moment I tried to imagine the two of us alone.

"I feel that I should be out on the range pushing cows," Sawtooth said, grinning sheepishly after his particularly ear-wrenching, off-key rendition of "Little Joe on the Prairie."

"Don't worry," I told him. "We'll more than make up for this little time of relaxation."

The clatter of hooves and butcher-knife wheels on the hardpan in front of the ranch house cut through our laughter. Frank glanced out the window. "I wonder what they want. It's Newt Adams and Williford Perkins." He snorted. "Perkins is dressed like he was going to a church meeting."

"Shoot, Frank," Peewee jeered. "That's how all

them rich folks dress, like they was going to a preaching meetin'.''

Cal looked at Carrie and then at me. ''You want me to let them in, boss?''

Carrie said, ''Yes, invite them in. We can all listen to what they have to say.''

Followed at a respectful distance by the sheriff, Perkins entered the parlor. His cold eyes took in the celebration without a flicker of surprise. He puzzled me. He was like no banker I had ever known. When his eyes reached me, a cruel grin curled his thin lips. He removed his hat and nodded to Carrie. ''Miss Alexander.'' I noticed that Perkins still wore no gun.

''Good evening, gentlemen. What brings you out here so late?'' Carrie asked.

Perkins's lips tightened. ''Business, Miss Alexander.'' He cut his eyes in my direction before continuing. ''My teller informed me that he extended your note today.''

''That's right,'' she replied. ''He explained that such an extension was routine.''

His lips twisted into a sneer. ''Once perhaps, but no longer. Following bank policy, I have not granted extensions on any loans for the last three years.'' He glanced at Newt Adams. ''I apologize for bringing the sheriff along, but I was uncertain of your reaction when I returned your money and insisted the note be paid in full—and on time. Understand me,'' he added hastily, ''I wish no trouble. All I want is what is legally due me.''

Carrie's hand flew to her lips, which parted in a silent scream.

I eyed Perkins narrowly. "Seems like a mighty convenient policy to me."

He matched my stare with cold, slate-gray eyes. "That's business, Mr. Colter."

I had looked into other eyes like his, eyes that spoke of death. I had never met a banker like him, and a shudder ran up my spine. "I can't say I like your kind of business, Mr. Perkins. Making a profit on the misfortunes of others is more in the line of thieves."

His jaw muscles twitched under the tightly drawn skin on his face. His eyes glittered with amusement, and he grinned. "If I don't, Mr. Colter, someone else will."

Carrie finally found her voice: "You're despicable."

He turned his mocking eyes on her. "Sorry you feel that way, Miss Alexander, but business is business." He paused, taking his time to fix his eyes on every man present. Finally, he said over his shoulder to Newt Adams, "Looks like we're ready to leave, Sheriff."

Adams nodded, replaced his hat, and stepped aside to let Williford Perkins pass.

Futility filled my veins with rage. "Hold it, Perkins!" I snapped.

The tall, lanky man's hand darted to his hip, then froze before moving less than six inches. Deliberately, although awkwardly, he brought his hand up to idly brush back his hair over his ear as he turned to face me. He arched an eyebrow, disdaining to respond to my sharp words.

I struggled to keep my voice soft and level, but it shook as I spoke: "You're as low a snake as I've ever known. You're legal now. I see that, but if you ever make a mistake, I'll jump in the middle of your back and stomp you to a grease spot."

For a moment, his restraint almost cracked. A blaze of fury flashed from his cold eyes, heating them to a blistering rage. But just as quickly, he smothered the fire. A cool grin revealed even, white teeth. "I make no mistakes, Mr. Colter."

Newt Adams snickered, but ducked his head when I glared at him.

After they had left, Carrie came up to me. I was still tense with anger, wanting to strike out with my fists and destroy whatever stood before me. She laid her hand on my shoulder.

When I looked at her, I saw a different woman— not the weak little calf from San Francisco, but a tough and determined woman who could stand alongside a man as they built a place for themselves.

"We still have two weeks," she said.

I looked at the crew scattered around the parlor. Ed stared at me from where he was leaning against the wall by the window. Two men stared at the floor. Sawtooth and Cal Stone looked me square in the eye, waiting for orders. I looked back at Carrie.

"Two weeks ain't no time at all," Ed said. "Might as well give it up." He nodded to Carrie and walked out of the parlor. The other crew members followed his lead.

When they were gone, she looked up at me, her face

taut with worry. "Can we do it?" She swallowed hard. "I mean, can we do it in time?"

Despite the hole we suddenly found ourselves in, I couldn't resist grinning. No longer was she a quitter. But, I reminded myself, she still had not faced some of the obstacles that had broken others, although she was certainly facing a major one now. I didn't know if we could meet the deadline or not, but one thing was for certain. If we didn't get the money in time, no one would ever be able to say we didn't try.

"We're going to give it a heck of a try!" I answered.

I slept but little that night. Rising early, I rode out on the range, where I did my best thinking. My first thoughts were to make a quick gather of beef and push them north. But such an endeavor would take too much time.

Perhaps I could contact John Tolbert, the buyer from Chicago, and sell him beef. We could deposit the funds in a Dodge bank while I drove the herd north. He could send a verification of deposit to the Sweetwater Creek Bank, a deposit Perkins would be forced to honor.

But such a sale would strip the Flying A of breeding stock, and even then, we couldn't pay off the mortgage. All we had was three hundred head, which at top dollar would bring three thousand. Even with the fifteen hundred, we would still be five hundred dollars short. And there was no way Williford Perkins would throw any slack in the rope.

The buckskin crossed the muttering creek, and I headed toward the canyons near the valley rim. The sun approached midsky when I topped out on the rim. In the distance, a herd of antelope, spooked by my sudden appearance, bounced across the prairie.

Shifting in the saddle and hooking my leg around the saddle horn, I paused to watch the graceful animals. As I followed their bounding leaps, a glimmer of red caught my eyes. It was one of the stakes I had seen months earlier.

Suddenly, I remembered what John Tolbert had said about the possibility of the railroad laying track through the Panhandle. Could that be what those stakes indicated? If so. . . .

I shook my head in disbelief. The possibilities connected with such an undertaking were endless. But how could I be certain?

My first thought was of John Tolbert. The only way I could get the information from him was by telegraph, but Perkins was a powerful man in Sweetwater Creek, and if I sent Tolbert a wire requesting such information, the banker would learn of it within minutes. I knew I might be chasing the wind, but I didn't want Perkins to know my plan. I wanted him to believe we were hard-thrown and hog-tied.

Riding to Dodge was out of the question. The round trip would take five or six days—if any horse could stand up to the rigors of such a journey. And the trip might be for nothing, because there was always the possibility that the stakes had nothing to do with the railroad. And if that happened to be the case, I would have wasted six days that I might have been able to use more profitably.

No, I had to get the information locally, but the only man who would know was Williford Perkins. And he would laugh in my face if I asked him.

I pulled the buckskin around and headed back into the valley. That's when I remembered the bank clerk Perkins had fired. The poor jasper would probably be eager to spill whatever he knew. Touching my spurs to the buckskin's flank, I headed for town. I said a short prayer that the ex-clerk would possess the information I sought.

A hostler directed me to the white bungalow on the outskirts of town. Markby was home, and he looked me square in the eye as I explained my situation as we sat in his parlor.

"I understand exactly what you're asking," he said. "Were I still in the employ of the Sweetwater Creek Bank, I could say nothing. But since I am without employment at the present, I see no reason not to provide you with the information you seek."

"So you do know something about the survey on the valley rim?"

He nodded and ran his slender fingers through his thinning hair. "Yes. At least, I think I do. One day about three years ago, I returned to the bank after hours to catch up on the day's work. It had been an unusually busy day. Apparently, Mr. Perkins didn't hear me enter even though his office door was open."

He hesitated and arched an eyebrow, wondering if I understood the implication. I nodded, and he continued. "I busied myself at my desk, posting debits and credits, you understand, when I overheard Mr. Perkins use the word 'rich.' Naturally, that caught my attention.''

"Naturally," I commented.

Markby forced a weak grin and continued. "They were speaking of railroads, and I heard Mr. Perkins ask if a survey had been done. His visitor replied that one had indeed been completed. He also added this was an opportunity that came once in a man's life.'' Markby grinned sheepishly. "I'm not a brave man, Mr. Colter, and suddenly I was frightened that I would be discovered. Such a discovery could have proved very embarrassing. So I left the bank.''

"Did Perkins hear you?"

"If he did, he said nothing of it.'' He glanced out the window and lowered his voice. "Perhaps it was just an overactive imagination on my part, but Mr. Perkins just never seemed to fit into the mold of a banker.''

His observation brought my own questions concerning the banker rushing into my mind. "How do you mean?" I leaned forward in my chair and rested my elbows on my knees.

He shook his head. "I don't know. I've worked in banks all my life, and he just seems out of place.''

I knew how he felt, for the same nagging worry had tormented me. "Did he say where the railroad ran its survey?''

"No. I'm sorry.''

I rose and extended my hand. "Don't be, Mr.

Markby. You've been mighty helpful, more than you know. What are your plans now?''

A sad smile played over his face. "Who knows? Banking is all I know. I'm no cowboy. I'll find something," he said. "Don't worry."

After I left his modest house, pieces of the puzzle began falling into place. C.H. had told me that Perkins came in a few years back and began buying up everything in sight. That took time and money, vast sums of money. Just how high must the stakes be for a man to invest years of his life and large sums of money in such a gamble? Probably higher than a cowpoke like me could imagine.

On the way back to the ranch, I pieced together a plan. If Perkins could reap a fortune from the railroad, why couldn't Carrie? All I had to do was find out if the Atchison or whichever line was pushing rails into the Panhandle, contact them to arrange a deal, and get the money back to Sweetwater Creek in less than two weeks.

I knew that the plan was a long shot, but looking down the road, I didn't see any other choice. There certainly wasn't anyone out there beating down our doors with money to pay off the mortgage.

In order for me to carry out my plan, Carrie suggested I needed legal power of attorney, not just a handwritten note. Since Sweetwater Creek had only one lawyer, we had no choice, although I knew that as soon as our dust had settled, the shyster would make certain that Williford Perkins knew of the transaction.

And such a transaction, even if the banker was unaware of the specifics, was certain to arouse his curiosity as well as his wariness.

Ed packed hardtack, jerky, and a few cans of tomatoes in my saddlebags, and I, with all the necessary legal documents, rode out on the buckskin leading two sound horses, so that I could switch and always keep a fairly fresh horse under me. I made good time to the Canadian River, where I put the horses out to graze while I napped from midnight until about three. Then I rose and struck out again. Usually, Indians did not travel at night unless they had a good reason, but I kept my eyes peeled.

On the crest of a sand hill, I pulled up and studied a blazing fire a couple of miles below in a sprawling valley. It was too large to be Indian.

But I took no chances. The Texas Panhandle was a vast, empty land, and a man had no idea who he might run into, so he had to play his cards close to the vest. Comancheros could be sitting around the blaze, and they were worse news than even the Comanche. On the other hand, the hombres camped there could be cowpokes just like me, and hungry for another gun for added security.

Although I would reach Indian Territory by sunrise and the company of others would be reassuring, I could take no chances on whoever was sitting around the fire. And so I swung wide, keeping the night breeze in my face.

Just before dawn I left the last of the sand hills behind and topped out on the northeastern edge of the Staked

Plains. As flat and dry as burned pancakes, the plains offered no shelter, no protection from either the elements or enemies. The grass was dry and brittle. A chill of premonition ran up my spine. This area was where we had given beef to the Indians during our cattle drive.

Switching mounts, I headed across the plains in a gentle but mile-eating lope. The miles fell behind. I was beginning to relax, because a more hospitable countryside awaited me in a few hours.

Just before noon a dark line appeared on the horizon, the North Canadian River. Suddenly, the roan I forked stumbled, but caught itself and came up limping. Dismounting, I checked his leg. The cannon bone felt sound, but I felt a slight swelling around the fetlock joint. Nothing was broken, but the roan might have stretched a ligament. As I knelt, I felt a vibration in the hard-packed soil.

Dust billowed over the prairie to the east, stretching for miles along the horizon. Rising, I studied the dust cloud. Only one thing could cause a dust cloud so immense, could shake the ground like an earthquake— a runaway herd of buffalo. And about the only reason for the normally sluggish animals to stampede was men on horseback—Indians. The white man didn't need to run the buffalo; they just perched on a hill and killed them by the hundreds.

Without bothering with a saddle, I swung onto the buckskin and dug my heels into his flanks. I glanced at the swing of trees lining the North Canadian and then back at the billowing dust. A faint black line appeared at the base of the cloud.

I knew I could outrun the buffalo. That was not a concern. My concern was evading the eyes of the men behind the herd.

I reached the river with ease and pulled into a grove of cottonwood to watch the passing herd less than a mile south of me. From where I sat on the buckskin, I saw only one flank of the herd, but I knew that if my vantage point were higher, I would see a blanket of black stretching to the southern horizon, thundering across the prairie.

As the herd swept past, six riders broke away and headed in my direction. I muttered a curse and looked around for some kind of fortification for myself and my animals. A hundred yards downriver, a bulwark of drift logs was piled on a sandbar in the middle of the river, giving me a clear field of fire for fifty yards on all sides. Enough room for me, but not for my horses. On the river's edge grew a plum thicket, which was a poor shelter but better than none. Quickly hobbling and securing the horses in the middle of the thicket, I grabbed my Winchester and saddlebags and climbed into the tumble of driftwood and took refuge behind a thick log.

Just as I ducked behind the log, a rifle boomed and a slug whined above my head. Levering a round into the chamber, I peered over the log and saw two braves astride wiry little ponies heading toward me. Comanche. The jingling bells tied to their saddles gave them away. They waved rifles over their heads, probably some old .50 caliber Sharps taken from unfortunate soldiers and travelers.

I jerked my saddle gun to my shoulder and squeezed off a shot. The slug caught the rearmost brave in the chest and somersaulted him backward out of the saddle. The second one fired and I ducked.

Several more slugs whined past as the other braves joined in the fight. There were at least five out there. The only advantage I had was my cover and their poor weapons. Slugs ripped slivers and chunks from the log. I crawled to the end of the log where the current had washed debris under the log, forming a thick blind. I managed to clear enough debris so that I could see without exposing myself to any fire.

The Comanches remained hidden and fired periodically. Obviously, they were in no hurry. Suddenly, my buckskin and my other two mounts stampeded up the riverbank pursued by a yelling Indian on horseback. I snapped off a shot and knocked him off his pony. He hit the ground and scrabbled for cover, dragging a leg behind him.

But now I was in a fix. Without horses, there was no way I could get to Dodge on time. All I could hope for now was to escape with a whole skin. I looked downriver and my hopes surged. If I could hold them off until night, maybe I could slip into the river and escape. But there were still several hours of daylight remaining.

Those hopes faded in midafternoon, when three more Comanches started firing from a sandbar downriver. Now I was surrounded.

Although old Ned had always joshed me by swearing that I would depart this world at the hands of angry Indians, which was the way my situation sure looked now, I wasn't particularly eager to give him the satisfaction of having the last word.

But my chances looked mighty glum. Come night, they would be moving in.

Distant gunfire echoed from upriver. My hopes sank. Looked like more were coming to get in on the fun. I checked my hardware. It appeared things were going to get mighty busy in the next few minutes.

I had not returned their fire for several minutes, and a couple of them were growing careless. One stuck his head up and glanced over his shoulder, giving me all the time I needed. I squeezed off a shot that caught him right between the eyes when he looked back around.

Another flurry of slugs raked the logs, but I stayed low and shoved in more bullets. The distant gunfire grew closer. I gripped the Winchester and tried to still the fear clogging my throat. To the west, the sun lit the sky with a golden glow. *Fitting*, I told myself. *It's the last one I'll see.*

The gunfire intensified, but strangely enough, no slugs whined past me. Downriver, the three Comanches leaped astride their ponies and made a mad dash for the thickets on the south shore. "What the devil is going on?" I muttered.

Peering over the log, I saw the Comanches scramble for cover among the cottonwoods as hard-riding Indians bore down on them. One of the mounted Indians looked around, and I ducked behind the log. My brain reeled with the sudden realization that the mounted Indians were Apache.

Maybe here was the help I needed to reach Dodge, but first I had to palaver with them before they came hunting me.

I remained motionless, my ears straining for any sounds of approach as the newcomers quickly routed the Comanches. Minutes later, when I heard a pony splashing through the shallow water, I peered through the tangle of underbrush beneath the log. The mounted brave was the same Apache who had looked around when I snapped off my last shot.

He paused thirty yards away, studying the tumble of driftwood. I called out to him in Apache, ''I am a friend.''

At my words, he stiffened and lowered the muzzle of his ancient carbine until it was centered on the drift-wood. ''You are white man.''

''Yes, but I am also of the White Mountain family.''

Without replying, he turned and slowly rode back to the other Apaches. For several moments they talked. Then he rode back as the others watched from the shore.

''What do they call you?''

''Colter. I was married to Morning Flower.''

Again he rode back. When he returned, another Apache accompanied him. The second brave looked familiar. ''White man!''

''I am here.''

The second Apache spoke, his tone revealing his skepticism: "Morning Flower is not of this world."

Then I remembered the brave's name. Holding my Winchester out to my side to show my friendliness, I rose slowly and nodded. "You speak true, Sharp Nose. Comancheros killed her four years ago. And I killed them."

The first Apache looked around in surprise at Sharp Nose, who smiled slowly and said, "We wondered if you caught them. Much time has passed, Colter. You look the same."

"You are well?" I responded.

He nodded. "Come. It is good that family eats and drinks together."

Night settled in on us like a black velvet cloak. Around the blazing fire, many memories returned, some pleasant but many filled with pain. The news Sharp Nose gave me brought more pain. Many of the White Mountain family were dead. The Apache nation was dying. Soon it would no longer exist. General George Crook had maintained a constant pressure on the Apache for the last few years, forcing many to reservations, killing many, and as in Sharp Nose's case, driving many from the territory.

I looked around the fire at the grim faces staring into the small fire. Each set of eyes saw different memories in the dancing flames, memories of what had been.

"Where do you go now?" I asked.

Sharp Nose shrugged. "Who can say? All we want is to be left alone. We have heard of a great wilderness far to the north."

My heart ached. He would never be permitted to live in peace, the white man would not permit him, but I could not say the words and destroy his hopes, for hopes were all that remained for Sharp Nose and the other Indians, no matter what their tribe.

"And you, Colter, where do you go?"

How I wished to speak of my dreams to another, but my Morning Flower was still too much in them. She had been dead these four years, but I was unable to truly accept the fact. When I could accept it, I could release her, and then perhaps I would find happiness once again.

So I simply replied, "Dodge City." And I told him of my mission.

The next morning Sharp Nose presented me with two tough little ponies. And we parted ways, each grasping the other's forearm in a firm clasp. I looked into his eyes, and he into mine, and we each knew we would never see the other again in this world.

I crossed the river and climbed out of the valley to the rim high above. There I paused and looked back. The Apaches ambled single file along the riverbank. They reached a bend. One stopped and looked back. He raised his hand, and I raised mine. And a part of my life was forever gone.

The Indian ponies were as wiry and durable as they were ugly and scrawny. I rode them hard, maintaining a full gallop to make up for lost time. At midday I crossed the Cimarron River and reached the Arkansas and Dodge by early morning.

At the hotel the sleepy clerk told me that John Tolbert had gone to Wichita for two weeks. Leaving the ponies at a livery, I hitched a train and rolled into Wichita several hours later. By three o'clock I had found Tolbert and explained what was taking place, and the two of us were on another train heading north to Abilene.

Not having been exposed to much of the legal machinery running the country, I harbored much skepticism. "And you say a deal like I'm proposing is possible," I asked Tolbert.

He grinned at me. "Not only possible, Mr. Colter, but in this case very likely."

I returned his grin and leaned back on the seat. I sure hoped he was right, and I believed I could trust the man, but now I reckoned on catching up on a heap of missed sleep.

In Abilene, Tolbert's prediction proved to be accurate. By the end of the day, I was on a train headed back to Dodge, wearing a money belt filled with brand-new bills, ten thousand dollars' worth.

I left Dodge and crossed the Arkansas River just before dusk, intending to put a few miles behind me before camping, for I figured I had five or six days before the mortgage was due. The Cimarron was fifty miles to the south and I wanted to reach the river by dusk of the next day.

At midnight I made a cold camp and slept until just before dawn. After a hasty breakfast of coffee and hardtack, I moved out. The day was hot and the air was dry. I made good time. Just before I reached the Cimarron, I reined into a thicket of scrub.

Far to the south, a thin vapor of dust rose into the clear sky. After dismounting, I loosened the cinch and let the ponies browse while I watched the dust. Soon a single line of riders appeared, heading east. As they grew closer, I saw they were Indians. They were too distant to discern which tribe, but I figured them to be Comanche. I checked my hardware in case they headed in my direction, but they continued east, angling slightly south to intersect the river.

I waited until they disappeared over the horizon and their dust had settled. When I finally moved out, it was at a gallop. I wanted to cross the Cimarron and put another ten or fifteen miles behind me before I camped.

Dusk was growing deeper when I reached the Cimarron, and without a pause I pushed the pony into the river. Suddenly, something clubbed my head, and I felt myself falling. As I slipped into unconsciousness, I heard the echoes of a rifle shot rumbling down the river.

Chapter Thirteen

The cold water shocked me. Desperately I struggled to keep from slipping into unconsciousness. The current tugged at me, pulling me with it as I struggled to keep my head above water. I opened my mouth to suck air into my starving lungs, but instead I swallowed a mouthful of water. I choked and gagged.

The vicious undertows and treacherous crosscurrents pulled me under the rushing water. I felt myself rolling across the rocky bottom, bouncing off submerged boulders, tumbling over water-soaked logs. Frantically I fought across the current and tried to reach the bank.

My fingers touched a root, and another, and then another. Cattails. I had reached shore. I felt a pile of broken twigs and dry grass, debris deposited by the river during its last flood. I could hide there. Suddenly, my fingers grasped air as I was swept farther downriver. Another sharp blow struck my head, and the last thing I remembered before slipping into unconsciousness was being slammed into some submerged branches and becoming entangled.

I awakened chilled to the bone, the water racing past

my throat. I tried to raise my head, but it struck something hard, like a rock. Still groggy, I closed my eyes and drew several deep breaths before opening them again.

I was under a large rock ledge that extended several feet over the river and only eight or nine inches above the surface. At some time earlier, an uprooted tree had been washed under the ledge, and it was in that tree's branches I had become tangled.

It was morning, but the overhang hindered my vision. I made out the cattails and the pile of debris into which I had tried to crawl the night before. Suddenly, a set of horse's legs entered my field of vision, followed by a second set.

Both sets stopped at the stack of debris. Gunfire erupted as the riders blew the pile apart. Beneath the echo of gunfire rolling downriver, I heard the mutter of voices, but the words were too indistinct. The horses continued upriver. Just as they rounded a bend and disappeared, I managed a glimpse of the trailing horse. It was an Appaloosa.

Jim Farley! His name fueled a burning rage in me, driving out the chill of the river.

I remained hidden for several minutes. Then I saw Farley again, far upriver where the Cimarron made a gentle *S* bend. He was followed by a second rider, and although they were too distant for me to discern the second rider's features, he had to be Bill Hollier.

I struck out across the river, knowing they could not see me at such a distance. Upon reaching the south shore, I headed across the prairie with no horse, no hat, no gun. My only weapon was my double-edged knife, given to me by Morning Flower's brother upon the announcement of our betrothal.

I glanced at my boots and wished for the more comfortable moccasins, which would permit me to travel much faster. Boots, after a few miles, tended to break down a man's arches. The best I could do was pry the heels off with my knife. When I wedged the point of the knife under my boot heel, I suddenly realized just how Bob Cook was killed. And I was fair certain who was behind Carrie's trouble. I just didn't know why.

Instinctively, I stayed in the gullies and arroyos, avoided sandy soil when I could, brushed out sign when it was too obvious. All this I did without conscious thought, which allowed me time to ponder the enigma of Jim Farley and Bill Hollier.

Somehow they had escaped the hangman, but how did they find out about me and this trip? From Perkins? Possibly, but the banker had been given no clue as to my destination. As far as he knew, I was heading for Chicago or San Francisco with the power of attorney.

That left the three people who knew my destination—Carrie, Ed, and Frank.

Ahead of me, a buzzard flapped his great, awkward wings and lumbered into the air at my approach. He caught some rising thermals and soared high above my head in great, slow circles, keeping a wary eye on his meal of carrion.

It was a buffalo. I wrinkled my nose at the stench. On the prairie, a man grows accustomed to death, both of man and animal. What I could not accustom myself to was the idea that one of the three people I held in high regard could be so devious, so calculating.

Late that afternoon, when a cloud of dust billowed on the horizon behind me, I dropped to my knees and studied the cloud. There was a possibility that the riders were not Jim Farley and Bill Hollier, but I would not have laid two bits on such a bet at even a hundred to one odds. I peered around for a place to hide, but as far as the eye could see was only grama and buffalo grass, with not even a hiding place large enough to conceal a prairie dog.

A hundred feet or so to my left lay a dead buffalo, its dried and brittle skin still stretched over its bones. I had no choice. Remaining in a crouch, I ran to the skeleton and, after checking for rattlesnakes hiding from the blistering sun, I crawled inside, hoping that neither of the men would decide to take some target practice.

Thirty minutes later I heard voices and the soft grunt of trudging horses. I looked through a rip in the dried skin. The two rustlers were less than fifty yards from me. I held my breath as they drew closer. If they continued on their present course, they would pass within thirty or forty feet of me.

Bill laughed and pointed at the buffalo skeleton. He drew his revolver, but Jim said something, and the loose-witted man holstered his gun.

I sighed with relief and closed my eyes, but a scraping sound caught my attention. I glanced around. My blood ran cold. Heading directly for the skeleton was some mighty unwelcome company—a rattlesnake as big around as my forearm.

Gathering a handful of sand, I tossed it at the serpent. The sudden movement of my hand and the sand striking the ground in front of the snake galvanized the serpent into a defensive posture. It coiled, and its buttons hummed.

I looked past the snake in alarm, hoping the two riders would not hear the snake and return to kill it. I remained motionless. After a few tense seconds, the snake eased from its coils and once again headed toward me.

By now, Bill and Jim were too far away to hear the snake, so I threw another handful of sand at it. And again it coiled and sang its song of death.

While it lay coiled, I took a chance and slipped out of the skeleton, more than willing to let the rattlesnake have it. Keeping my eyes on the two men, I lay on the ground several feet behind the buffalo, taking care to keep the brittle bones and dried skin between me and the two rustlers, and at the same time have room to maneuver should the rattler decide to bypass the buffalo.

It didn't. Through the rips and tears in the skin, I saw the serpent coil in the rump of the buffalo. I lay quietly, waiting for the sun to set.

I pushed out after dark, grateful for my boots now. The prairie at night is not for the unwary. The first couple of hours I moved slowly, trying to see what lay before me. About ten the moon rose, and I traveled faster then.

A few hours later I spied the shadowy line of trees marking the North Canadian. After fording the river, I drank my fill of water, dropped a couple of pebbles into my pocket, scavenged up a pocketful of cattail bulbs and several stalks, and turned to my next destination, the Canadian some fifty miles south.

As I journeyed, I wove the cattail stalks into a rough basket that I set on my head to ward off some of the sun's rays. The prairie began to roll, and by sunup, I was back among the sand hills and sagebrush. At noon I pulled up some sage and built a rough arbor to provide some shade, after which I lay down and napped until midafternoon.

I placed a pebble from the river under my tongue when I set out again. An old trick, it eased my thirst and moistened my throat. The woven basket kept my head fairly cool.

I saw no sign of Jim or Bill, but I avoided the skyline, taking care to skirt the hills and stay beneath their crests.

The hours dragged by. The sky overhead turned into a yellow bowl. Several times I staggered and fell, but I persisted. I had to reach the Canadian. Finally, the coolness of approaching evening blew across the prairie, refreshing me.

In the early hours of the morning, I reached the Canadian. I stumbled into the water and let it flow over me for what seemed like hours. I crawled out and hid in a plum thicket where I fell into a deep sleep.

I awakened with a start. The sky was gray with the approaching dawn. I lay motionless, trying to discern just what had awakened me, but the only sounds I heard were the birds chirping in the trees and the river as its waters bubbled and rushed over the rocks.

My body ached as I rose to my feet. After riding a horse for as long as I had, walking was an unaccustomed exercise. I found a few berries the birds had left and dug up a few roots. That and a bellyful of cool, sweet water knocked the hunger pangs out of my stomach for the time being.

I waded into the river and swam to the other side. I shivered when I climbed out, but I knew that the thirty miles I had left to travel would warm me up. I made my way through the cottonwood grove to the prairie.

Harsh words froze me. "Get those hands up, Colter!"

Bill Hollier stepped from behind a cottonwood and grinned at me, his .44 leveled at my belly. He had a dark bruise on his chin, and one eye was swollen and black. "Figured you'd be coming this way."

I glanced around.

"Don't worry. Jim'll be along. He's been mighty eager to see you." He laughed and gestured to a cottonwood. "Get over there and turn around."

I did as he said, looking desperately for a weapon of some kind. He jammed the muzzle in my back. "Put your hands behind you."

He gave me no choice. I followed his orders. Using one hand, he slipped a loop around one of my wrists and wrapped it around the other wrist several times, each time looping over and under and around my wrists. The job was awkward with one hand, but I figured he was afraid to put his gun down.

"Now sit down against the tree!" He strung a rope around the tree and over my chest two or three times. When he finished, he squatted in front of me and grinned. "Yep, old Jim is sure gonna be pleased to see you."

Trussed up like a calf ready for the branding iron, I replied, "Not as surprised as I am to see you with him, especially after he cheated you out of your share of the that money."

Bill's grin faded. "He explained that."

It was my turn to laugh. "I'll bet."

His face darkened in anger. "He did too."

I wasn't sure what good needling him would do. It might get me a boot in the teeth, but I had nothing else to try. "What kind of lie did he make up about the rest of the money?"

Hollier stood up and shook his head emphatically. "No lie. The two thousand was our share. The man who planned it all got the rest of the money. I told you, he lied to Jim. He told Jim that all he got was four thousand."

"Who's he?"

Bill eyed me slyly. "Never you mind."

"Come on, Bill," I said, shaking my head. "Even you can't believe that Farley would let someone cheat him. He's lying to you. Ask the gambling houses in Abilene. They'll tell you he gambled it away."

"You lie!" He glared at me, so angry he was shaking. Finally, he pivoted and stormed away. While he was gone, I worked desperately at the bonds on my wrists. I knew I was a dead man when Jim came back. Despite Bill's one-handed effort to tie my wrists, I couldn't loosen the bonds enough to free my hands.

I leaned forward against the rope holding me to the cottonwood. It gave some. I pushed forward again, and again the rope gave until it was loose enough for me to slide from under.

At that moment Bill returned leading his horse. He tied the animal to a nearby tree and unleathered his revolver. He fired three shots into the air, holstered his gun, and grinned at me. "Not long now, Colter."

I ran my tongue over my lips. "How about a drink at least."

He frowned. For a moment, I thought he was going to refuse, but he retrieved his canteen and leaned over and touched it to my lips.

I kicked him, driving the toe of my boot into the flesh beneath his jaw. He stumbled back, gagging and grabbing his throat. I slid from under the ropes and doubled my legs and body forward so that I could slip my bound wrists under my feet.

Bill fell, and I jumped him and grabbed for his revolver.

A shot rang out, and a slug ricocheted off a rock at my feet. I spun as Jim fired again. I leaped aside and squeezed the trigger.

The Appaloosa squealed and reared and fell on its side, sending Jim tumbling to the ground. Behind me, Bill jumped to his feet and raced through the cotton-woods downriver. Jim had rolled behind the cottonwood to which Bill had tied his own animal. He squeezed off two shots, jumped into the saddle, and raced away.

He was an elusive target among the cottonwoods. Once, I had a clear shot at the horse, but I did not fire. I would run into Jim again. First I had to reach the Flying A.

Not wanting to draw the town's attention to my arrival, I swung wide and took the back trail into the Flying A. That evening I paused at Sweetwater Creek to fill Bill's canteen and take a short breather before striking out for the last eight miles.

I lay on my belly and drank deeply from the creek. I had visions in my head of Carrie and me walking into the bank and counting out the cash to Williford Perkins.

The ice-cold click of a hammer being cocked froze me.

A sneering voice said, "Well, well, well. If it ain't Shadrach Colter, flat on his belly and five seconds away from hell."

I looked up. On the other side of the creek stood Jim Farley, a mocking grin on his thin lips and a wolf's leer in his eyes. "Right between the eyes, Colter."

I threw myself to the right and grabbed for my own six-gun as he fired. The roar of the .44 deafened me, and a stinging bite numbed my left shoulder. I rolled over and fired. Another explosion beat against my ears and dirt and sand blinded me. I kept rolling and firing at the spot where he had been standing. Then my hammer clicked on a spent cartridge.

But suddenly I realized that I had heard no return fire. I squinted against the sand and dirt in my eyes. Jim had disappeared. I looked again, and through the grass I saw the soles of his boots facing me. Quickly I ejected the spent cartridges and reloaded.

Cautiously rising into a crouch, I kept a wary eye on the inert figure lying in the grass. He lay arms outstretched and his face turned aside. Easing around, I looked into his face. His eyes were open, and his mouth gaped in shock. I looked again and realized that Jim Farley was dead.

Then I became aware of the numbing throb in my shoulder. My shirtsleeve was soaked with blood, and my shoulder burned as if someone had laid a hot running iron on it.

I washed the blood away and saw that the bullet had passed through the deltoid, that rounded clog of muscle on the outside of my shoulder. Blood flowed freely from the blue hole in my shoulder, which was good, for the flow would help cleanse the wound.

I found Jim's horse in a nearby thicket, and after a last look at the dead man, geehawed the horse toward the Flying A. I would send someone back to pick up the body.

As I rode, his last words played over and over in my mind: "Shadrach Colter, Shadrach Colter." Then I realized what had nagged at me ever since I read my full name signed to the power of attorney in Caldwell, Kansas. Only two men knew my given name. One of them was dead, and the other was already suspect. But there still remained the possibility that one of them had mentioned it to another party. In the back of my mind, a fuzzy plan sprang to life.

The orange ball of the sun balanced on the horizon, ready to roll off and drag the night across the sky behind it.

The handle of the Big Dipper in the northern sky was pointing to the northwest when I reached the ranch at about ten o'clock. The ranch was dark, but at the clip-clop of the horse's hooves on the hardpan yard, the squeak of the bunkhouse door cut through the still darkness.

A light shone through the front windows of the ranch house even before I stopped in front. From behind came the pad of bare feet.

"Colter! Is that you?" The voice belonged to Frank Ruffner. Behind him, Ed Boswell muttered something, but I couldn't make it out.

"Yeah," I replied, sliding off the horse. "It's me."

The front door opened, and Carrie came out carrying a lamp before her. "Oh, Shad, I'm so glad you're—" Her words choked off when she saw the condition I was in, but she didn't miss a lick. "Ed, Frank, help him inside the house! Hurry! Hurry!"

I was too exhausted to try to figure out which of the three was the traitor, and the soft couch under me did nothing to keep me awake. I must have dozed while Carrie tended my shoulder, for the next thing I remember, Frank was sticking a steaming mug of thick, black coffee in my hands. I felt some of my strength returning, but that couch still looked mighty inviting.

When Carrie saw that I was coming around, a right fetching smile played over her lips. "You know," she said, "you had us so worried, we forgot to ask about the trip."

"Yeah!" Frank exclaimed. "What about it, Shad? You get the money?"

Ed moved closer so that he could hear.

I reached under my shirt and pulled out the money belt and slapped it down on the coffee table. "Here it is, ten thousand, brand-new bills."

Carrie squealed with happiness, and Frank pounded Ed on the back. "Can't you just see Williford's face when we take him the money tomorrow?" she asked, her voice animated with delight.

All I could do was nod. I was so tired, I couldn't even make myself speak. My head jerked back in a nod, and Carrie ordered Frank and Ed to take me into the spare bedroom. "I'll look after him," she said.

I shook my head and struggled to my feet. I couldn't stay in the house, not if I wanted to carry out the plan I had put together. "I'm fine. The bunkhouse is okay."

She looked at me, distress in her eyes. "Are you sure?"

Her concern gave me a warm feeling. "Yeah. I'm fine." I nodded to the money. "Just put it up in a safe place."

"If you're sure." She reached for the money belt. "Tomorrow is the last day. We'll go into town and pay off the mortgage."

Somewhere I had lost a day or two. "I got back just in time, huh?"

She nodded, her eyes glistening with tears. The last words I heard her say were, "I'll put the money in the desk. It'll be safe there."

I awakened with a start sometime later. The bunkhouse was silent. Without waking anyone, I quickly dressed and slipped outside. After taking care of the little task I had set out to do, I hid in the undergrowth some distance from the main house.

The ranch was still and quiet. Only the distant wailing of coyotes broke the silence. I watched the house. All the ingredients to trap the traitor were present— the money, the time, and the opportunity. Whoever the traitor was, he had to make a move tonight. Tomorrow would be too late.

I struggled to remain awake, but the days of riding and walking were tough to overcome. Several times I dozed. Once I dropped my head, and something stung my cheek. I reached out to touch some of the undergrowth and jerked my hand back. I must have been beat, I realized. I had picked a bed of bull nettles to hide in. I tried to ease back from the stinging plants, but one stung my leg. I remained motionless, waiting for the traitor to give himself or herself away.

Owls swooped low and crickets chirruped. Once, I thought I heard an alien sound, but it didn't recur, so I dismissed it. That was my first mistake. Next, a shadow moved near the ranch house.

I squinted into the darkness. My vision blurred. Suddenly my head exploded with a thousand bursts of fireworks, and then I felt myself slipping into the depths of unconsciousness.

Carrie's screams cut into the black veil shrouding me. I struggled to shake off the lethargy holding me down. I stumbled to my feet, my head pounding and my senses groggy.

Carrie screamed again. I looked at the ranch house, and my blood ran cold. Flames leaped from the roof high into the night sky, lighting the darkness like day. Carrie screamed again. She was trapped. And in that moment I released Morning Flower to rest forever with her mother and father, and *Tapida*, the dawn, and *Chigonaay*, the sun.

As I raced across the hardpan, I saw Frank and Ed, followed by the rest of the crew, burst out of the bunk-house. At a dead run I leaped on the porch, lowered my shoulder, and slammed through the front door into a parlor raging with flames. The flames licked and snapped at me, but I didn't slow my speed. I threw myself at the bedroom door, which shattered from its jamb when I struck it.

Carrie was pressed against the outside wall, her eyes wide with fear. I grabbed a chair and hurled it through the window. Next I grabbed a sheet, threw it around Carrie, scooped her up, and handed her through the window to Cal Stone.

I followed her out the window. By now, the house was an inferno. Frank suddenly shouted, "The money! The ten thousand is inside!"

He lunged for the house, but I threw my arms around him. "Don't do it, Frank. It's too late. You wouldn't stand a chance." Even as I spoke, the roof fell in on the parlor and the desk where Carrie had placed the money for safekeeping.

With a sob, Carrie threw herself into my arms, her tears wetting my shirt.

By dawn, only a blackened chimney protruded starkly from the pile of smoldering coals. The leaves of the spreading oak were curled and brittle.

In the bunkhouse Peewee pulled out his meeting-day clothes for Carrie, who had lost every stitch of her clothing in the fire except for the nightgown she wore. But at least she was alive.

After she changed, we all sat silently around the table in the chuck house. I racked my brain trying to figure out who had started the fire—Ed or Frank. The fire itself eliminated Carrie.

"How about some more coffee, Ed?" Frank said.

Deep in thought, Carrie stared at the table without saying a word. Ed crossed to the stove for the pot. One of my hands tingled and I rubbed it. It was covered with red welts from the bull nettles. I glanced at Ed's worn wool trousers when he returned. Hundreds of tiny, white needles clung to the wool around his ankles. Suddenly I knew the identity of the renegade.

And then several pieces of the puzzle fell into place, beginning with the frown on C.H.'s face that first day when he told me about Ed.

But why? That's what I couldn't figure. C.H. had

known, and that's probably one of the reasons he was murdered.

When Ed finished pouring Frank's coffee, he held up the pot. "Anyone else?"

I shook my head. "No, but you might tell us just why you started the fire last night, Ed."

He froze. His face looked as if he had been struck right between the eyes with a twelve-pound sledge-hammer. As one, the entire crew looked at me in stunned disbelief.

"Shad! What are you saying?" Carrie cried, her voice filled with disbelief.

Ed just stared at me. The surprise fled his face, and a murderous hatred filled his eyes.

I continued: "After Ed knocked me out last night, he started the fire."

He laughed. "You're loco, tetched in the head."

"Am I?" I nodded to his pants. "Look. Full of bull nettles, or what some of you call stinging nettles. He got them when he cold-cocked me last night." I held up my hand for all to see. "I hid in the nettles to watch the house. You can see where they stung me."

Before I could say more, Ed launched the pot through the air, spraying us with coffee as he grabbed for his gun. The pot struck my arm, causing me to drop my revolver.

He grabbed Carrie and jammed the muzzle of his gun against her temple. "Don't no one move. I'll blow her purty head off."

We all froze in midstride. "Easy, Ed," I said. "You're playing a pat hand."

Carrie's face paled with fear.

Cal Stone edged apart from us. "He won't shoot, Shad. He's a gutless old man."

"Forget it, Cal," I said, deliberately keeping my voice low. "He's not as harmless as you think. He's the one who killed Bob Cook."

Ed grinned. "So you figured that out, did you?

I nodded. "Finally. Too bad you didn't use some of that horse sense the right way instead of like this."

His face darkened in anger. "Don't try to feed me no bad grain. I learned the hard way when Jimmy Alexander cheated me out of my share of this spread. I never forgot, neither."

Carrie caught her breath, and I finally discovered the motive that had evaded me. I said to Ed, "From all C.H. told me about the old man, that doesn't seem likely."

His eyes flared with defiance. "You think it don't? Well, you wasn't there early on when the spread come down on hard times. I gave Jimmy what money I had and agreed to work without pay for a share. We even shook on it. But when the cards started going his way, he gave me back my money and forgot about the hand-shake."

He became grim. "That was my one chance to be someone, not just another everyday, crippled-up range cook." He shook his head. "Jimmy stole my share, and I swore I'd get it back. Now, with the money burned up, I'm going to get what I deserve. And Jim Alexander can spin in his grave for all I care." He shot Peewee a sharp glance. "Bring me a horse—and be fast about it!"

Peewee looked at me, and I nodded. "Do as he says."

Ed giggled nervously. "Bet your boots you all goin' to do what I say."

"I figured you might be behind all our trouble, Ed, but I couldn't bring myself to admit it. You lied about Farley up in Caldwell. The bartender told you about him. You had me fooled."

He smirked. "Too bad for you, ain't it?" He waved the muzzle of his revolver, gesturing us to the far end of the chuck house. "Now you ain't going to be able to do nothing about it."

Cal Stone spoke up: "There's five of us who'll swear to what you admitted."

"You still don't get it, do you, knothead? We got the bank, and we got the sheriff on our side. You got nothing. The townsfolk'll gossip like old hens for a few days, but they won't do nothing. They never do."

Frank started to retort, but I interrupted him. "Hold on, Frank. Ed's right. Sometimes you win, sometimes you lose. I reckon this is our time to lose."

Frank looked at me as if I'd been eating locoweed.

Peewee came in and nodded to Ed. "Okay, the horse is outside."

Frank spoke up: "You might think you got us, Ed, but we'll be coming to town for you. You can bet your life on that."

"Come ahead. We'll be waiting. We'll all be waiting,'' he flung back defiantly, and he slammed the door behind him.

Cal Stone lunged for the closed door, but I stopped him. He spun on me angrily. ''Why'd you do that? I mighta got him.''

I shook my head. ''I want him to get away.''

Carrie stared at me in disbelief. ''You *what?*''

''He doesn't know about this,'' I said as I reached inside my shirt and pulled out the money belt and tossed it on the table.

Carrie recoiled from the belt, her eyes wide with fear. Frank looked at me and said, ''But—how did you—I thought it burned.''

''Not quite,'' I began, then hesitated. Carrie's reaction to the money puzzled me, but despite that, I nodded at the fading sounds of hoofbeats. ''I didn't want the guilty one to know we still had the money.''

Quickly, I explained how I had slipped back into the house and taken the belt. ''I knew someone had to make a move, and I didn't trust the money with anyone except me.'' I hesitated and grinned sheepishly at Frank. ''I figured the guilty one was either you or Ed. I figured Ed because only him and C.H. knew my full name, the name Jim Farley used up in Caldwell, Kansas. And then, when I figured out how Bob Cook was killed, I was fair certain Ed was the guilty party.''

Cal frowned. ''I don't understand.''

''The killer couldn't have been Frank, because he and Peewee stood guard together,'' I explained.

''Yeah,'' Peewee said. ''But we heard Bob moving around after Ed left.''

I shook my head. "No, you heard dishes fall, and you figured he was moving around."

Frank pursed his lips skeptically. "How'd Ed do it, then?"

I glanced at Carrie, who stood apart from us, eyeing each of us woodenly. Something was bothering her. Perplexed by her behavior, I kept glancing at her as I related the rest of my theory. "After he killed Bob Cook, Ed balanced the picket on the edge of the table, half on, half off. On the table end, he placed a cup full of water. He used a knife and punched a tiny hole in the bottom of the cup. On the end sticking off the table, he stacked the empty tins. After the water drained from the cup, the pie tins outweighed the empty cup, and they fell to the floor, making you think Cook was still alive."

"Well, I'll be!" Frank muttered. "That sneaky little varmint!"

"Sneaky maybe, but you can bet he'll have men on his side when we reach town," I said, unleathering my revolver and checking the cylinder. I slid the Colt back into the holster and faced the others. "I figure it's about time for us to make that final payment on the ranch."

Carrie's sudden outburst stunned us: "No! It's all over! You hear me? No more! No more killing!"

I turned to her in surprise. I had figured she would be the one most eager to even the score. "What are you talking about?"

She sat down at the table and stared at an empty coffee cup. "I'm quitting. Perkins can have this place." She looked up at us, her face twisted in anger.

"You're all savages out here. I thought I could fit in, but I can't. It's too brutal, too violent." She shook her head a few times. "I'm taking Perkins up on his offer."

Despite my feelings for her, I had finally had my fill, and I reached for the money belt. "Not yet you aren't."

She looked up at me in surprise. Behind me Frank muttered something. "What do you mean?" she demanded, her eyes cold, her face hard.

Shaking the belt in her face, I said. "I swore to C.H. I'd get this spread free of Williford Perkins. I'm going to do that. Then you, missy, can do whatever you choose, because as soon as I put the mortgage to the Flying A in your hands, I'm riding out of here."

She grabbed for the belt. "No! That's mine! Give it to me!"

I yanked it away from her. "Forget it, Miss Alexander," I said harshly. I pulled out five thousand and stuffed it in my pocket. I tossed the belt on the table before her. "I'm going to the bank."

I glanced at Cal and Sawtooth, who eyed her coldly. "Get the horses," I ordered them. "We got a date in town that won't keep."

Just before we reached town, I looked at the grim-faced riders behind me. "Boys," I said over my shoulder, "when I fight, I fight sudden. Watch me and stay ready."

Chapter Fourteen

The brim of my hat shaded my eyes against the blistering sun that baked the earth in a white glare. In the distance, Sweetwater Creek wriggled in the contorted images drawn by the rising thermals of heat. I massaged my stiff left shoulder.

No one spoke. The only sounds were the grunts of the horses and the clatter of hooves on the hardpan road. Even from this distance, I could tell that Ed Boswell and his men were waiting, because the main street, which normally bustled with noontime traffic, was empty.

At the edge of town, Frank and the others pulled up beside me until we rode abreast. We headed down the empty street toward the bank. Frightened faces peered at us from the windows.

Six men pushed through the batwing doors of the saloon on our right and sauntered into the street to head us off. One was the young one called Red, the deputy sheriff who had hurrahed me that first day in town, but now he wore no badge. Behind him came the same two rowdies who had been with him. Ed Boswell and

Newt Adams stepped through the door and stopped on the porch.

A hatchet-faced man with a day-old beard pushed past Red to face me. "That's far enough, Colter." Red stayed by his side as the others spread, their eyes locked on us, their fingers flexed, poised to leap for their revolvers.

I pulled up. Without taking my eyes from the leader of the gunnies, I spoke to Ed. "What's wrong, Ed? Afraid to handle your own troubles?"

He laughed. "I ain't no dummy, Colter. I know when I'm overmatched."

Faces watched the confrontation from behind windows. Going up against a sheriff, any sheriff, was right touchy. The onlooking citizens needed to know just where Newt Adams stood.

"What about you, Sheriff?" I asked. "You appear to be on the wrong side of the law this time. This just a memory lapse, or what?"

He shrugged and yanked his badge from his chest and tossed it on the boardwalk. "I wore that hunk of tin for five years to set all this up. I stand to make more in the next six months than I would for the next twenty years toting a badge."

I kept my eyes on the hatchet-faced man. "Well, I see you found garbage like yourself for company."

A cruel grin ticked up one side of Hatchet Face's lips.

I knew that if we attempted to dismount, none of us would touch the ground alive. We were at a disadvantage in attempting to outdraw them from the saddle, but when the firing began, our horses would spook, making us almost impossible targets, at least for the first few seconds of the battle.

"Cal, you take the jasper on the outside right." In a slow, relaxed voice, just as if I were reading a newspaper aloud, I then told the others whom to hit. "I'll take this ugly one in front of me and the one on his left. Now!"

Surprised, Hatchet Face recognized my intent too late and grabbed for his gun. I shucked leather and caught him in the middle of the chest before he could raise his gun. Spooked by the gunfire, my horse bolted and I missed Red with my next shot.

By then, everyone was firing. Explosions echoed around me as I snapped off a shot at a kneeling cowboy and knocked him on his back in the middle of the dusty street.

As suddenly as the firing began, it ceased.

I looked around. Three of the six lay motionless. The others lay moaning, clutching arms and chests.

Two of ours were injured: Cal Stone, whose gun arm hung limply at his side, broken, and Sawtooth, who lay on the ground, his head twisted at an awkward angle, his neck broken when he was thrown from his horse.

The clatter of footsteps on the boardwalk made me look up in time to see Ed and Newt Adams disappear into the bank.

"Okay, boys," I said. "Time to stick our boots

on solid ground. We're ready to cut stock for keeps.''

There were three of us now. We paused in the middle of the dusty street to reload, never taking our eyes off the bank for more than a glance. I pulled my hat down to cut out the glare of the sun, which reflected off the great expanse of windows across the front of the bank. I knew that both Ed and Perkins were inside, watching. But how many more gunsels did they have with them? That I didn't know.

The three of us—me, Frank, and Peewee—headed for the bank, shoulder to shoulder. Dust swirled about our feet, and sweat rolled down our cheeks. A sickening knot twisted in my stomach. Any man who says he is not afraid in a situation like this is a liar.

Although I kept my eyes fastened on the bank, I was aware of the brilliant blue sky above, cloudless, without a breath of air. How I would have loved to be lying on a grassy bank beside a mountain stream instead of where I was.

The only sounds breaking the silence were the jingling of spurs and the scuffing of boot heels in the sand. My eyes moved continuously, expecting the windows to explode with buckshot, or men to burst through the doors in a blaze of gunfire at any instant.

I stopped in the middle of the street in front of the bank. Rotating my shoulders once or twice, I drew a deep breath and tried to still the hammering of my heart against my chest. My voice echoed down the empty street: "I'm here to pay off the mortgage, Perkins.''

The door opened slowly, and Williford Perkins, now coatless, stepped onto the boardwalk. His hat brim was pulled down to shade his eyes, and double gun belts hung low on his narrow hips. Ed Boswell and Sheriff Newt Adams followed, one on either side of the banker. Perkins said, "Well, now, Mr. Colter, that's a right nice trick if you can do it, especially seeing as your money burned up."

Slowly I patted my pocket with my left hand. "Sad mistake, Perkins. The money didn't burn after all." I taunted Ed with a smirking grin. "I figured someone would try to get rid of the money, so I held on to it for safekeeping. And I reckon we're coming into your bank, one way or another."

"Your mistake, Colter, your last one," Ed cackled. He nodded to the banker, whose eyes continued to bore into mine. "This gent's real name ain't Williford Perkins. It's Doc Slater."

Peewee caught his breath, and Frank exclaimed, "Doc Slater!"

I shuddered with a sudden chill as I studied the gunfighter. He wore a crooked grin on his lips. From all I had heard, this wiry hombre facing me was the fastest gun alive, claiming over thirty notches on his handle.

His grin thinned as he nodded to the street behind me. "I've heard of you, Colter, and I saw you out there. You're fast. But you aren't fast enough."

I didn't hesitate in my reply, but it exuded a whole lot more confidence than I felt. Since I was going up against Slater, I figured I was bound to take some slugs, and I just hoped I could get a couple of good ones in before he did too much damage. "Maybe not, Doc, but you'd better make sure you stop me fast or I'll take you with me." A shadow of a frown flickered over his granite-hard face. He was not used to men defying him.

Peewee took one slow step sideways. "I'll take the sheriff."

Frank spoke directly to the cook: "Good. That leaves Ed for me. I wouldn't have it any other way, you backbiting coyote."

Slater's eyes remained glued to mine. For a second they flicked toward Peewee. That's when I made my move.

My hand darted for the .44 as I dropped into a crouch. He was faster than I thought. His gun appeared as if by magic in his hand before mine was leveled. In the next instant, well before the others cleared leather, orange explosions of fire belched from both our muzzles, hurling slugs across the twenty feet separating us.

His first slug caught me in the calf, spinning me around and to the ground. I hit and rolled over, cocking the hammer and firing as quickly as I could, hoping that my first shot had been true. Slater took a step toward me, flames spurting from his six-gun.

The thought that I had missed flashed through my mind as Slater continued firing. A slug tugged at my shirt, another stung my ear. I clenched my teeth and squinted into the smoke as the booming of six-guns reverberated through the air and deafened me. If I went out, Slater was going with me. I heard Peewee grunt and from the corner of my eye, saw him spin and fall headlong in the street. Dust billowed from the impact of his body. It mixed with the thickening smoke to sting my eyes.

Another slug tore up the ground in front of my face, stinging my eyes with grains of blinding sand. I forced my eyes open against the grinding pain. All I could make out was a vague image of Slater standing before me. Through the sudden silence in the street came the click of a hammer being cocked. Instinctively, I rolled aside as a six-gun roared. A moment later I heard the thud of a body hit the street.

The firing ceased. My ears rang. I lay motionless, my gun trained on the sprawled form of Doc Slater. Off to my left, Peewee moaned. He was alive, thank God.

I rose to my feet, rubbing the sand from my eyes. Unscathed, Frank remained in a crouch, his smoking gun leveled and waiting.

Doc Slater lay half in the street and half on the boardwalk, his slender fingers still grasping his revolver. My first shot had caught him in the heart, but the doomed man didn't know he was dead. He had one round remaining in the chamber, which meant he had squeezed off at least four shots with his heart blown apart.

Ed slumped on the boardwalk, his back leaning against the facade of the bank. His chin rested on his chest, just above two large stains on his shirt. Newt Adams lay face-down in the dirt.

*   *   *

At the insistence of Frank Devers and other prominent citizens, William Markby, the ex-bank clerk, took the final mortgage payment on the Flying A and agreed to manage the bank until the town council decided how best to legally handle the matter.

Back at the ranch the next day, we sat in the chuck house and drank stiff, black coffee. Cal's arm was in a sling, but his other arm was busy dunking Carrie's leftover doughnuts. Peewee hobbled around on crutches. As for me, a cane was a big help. Frank was the only one to come through without a scratch, so the job of ranch greasy belly naturally fell on his shoulders, a task he undertook with no small amount of misgiving.

"Best you jaspers gonna get from me is bacon and beans," he muttered.

Cal and Peewee laughed. I glanced at Carrie, who sat aloof at one end of the table, staring at the deed and title in her hand. I had planned to ride out after handing her the documents, but the slug through my calf had kept me overnight. I was ready to leave now.

It was a sad feeling to sit there with honest and loyal compadres and know I was leaving them, but my time had come, I reckoned. If I was ever to find that spread I had dreamed about, and to put down deep, solid roots, I had to be moving on.

But to be honest with myself, I had to admit that Carrie was the one I would miss most of all, despite the way she shilly-shallied from one position to the next, blowing hot and blowing cold. But I could understand what made her act that way—the West.

The West frightened many people. It was so vast that some folks just couldn't handle it. They had grown comfortable looking out the window and seeing a streetlamp on the corner, and one on the next corner, and one on the next. They felt secure in their own little part of the world. But when they peered across hundreds of miles of prairie and saw nothing but tumbleweeds and sage, they were lost.

That's what had happened to Carrie, and for the first time in my life, I cursed the West. It had driven away that which I had come to desire.

I glanced around the chuck house, taking it all in one more time, figuring I had put off my good-byes as long as I could. I drained the last of Frank's coffee, and though it was as vile as any I'd ever swallowed, it would always be in my thoughts on those cold nights when a man sits before a cheery blaze and reflects on all the good that has come his way.

The scraping of boots on the wood floor cut into my thoughts. Frank was herding Cal and Peewee out of the chuck house. At the door, Frank winked at Carrie and grinned at me.

Now what?

Carrie cleared her throat. "Shad?" Her face was pale and drawn.

I narrowed my eyes. If she thought I was going to sit here and listen to her complain any longer, she had another thought coming. "What now?" I asked.

She took several deep breaths. Her bottom lip quivered, and she nipped at it with her even, white teeth. "Don't go," she whispered. Before I could reply, she continued. "I know I'm headstrong and temperamental. I'm bullheaded one day and blow with the wind the next. I need someone to ride beside me."

I wasn't really sure just what she wanted to say, but my heart pounded a little faster when I tried to guess. "You can hire someone for that, someone that'll do whatever you tell 'em to do."

Her pale cheeks colored, and anger flashed through her eyes, but she held on to her temper. She studied me several seconds, and a rueful smile played across her lips. "You're bound and determined not to make it easy for me, aren't you?"

She lost me then. "What are you talking about now?" I asked.

Shaking her head, she sat next to me and laid her hand on mine. "I want you to stay, Shad." She laid the title and deed on the table before me. "I want us to spend the rest of our lives together. But you must understand this: If you stay and then later decide you want to pull up stakes and settle somewhere else, I'll follow you, whether you like it or not."

Finally, I saw some of old Jimmy Alexander's grit shine through in her like a full moon over the open prairie, and I liked what I saw. "It won't be easy."

She gazed out the open door to the prairie. Her eyes took on a faraway look. "Maybe not, but if we're together, it will be the only life for me." I looked into her eyes.

Somewhere well beyond the distant horizon, on a sunlit mountain peak high in the heavens, Morning Flower paused in her journey and looked back. She smiled with happiness and waved me good-bye.